To Don!
Best Wishes,
Jerome Art

One And Two Halves

An Anthology

Jerome Arthur

EAN: 978-0-9842990-5-8
ISBN: 0-9842990-5-X

Published by Jerome Arthur
P.O. Box 818
Santa Cruz, California 95061
831-425-8818
www.JeromeArthurNovelist.com
Jerome@JeromeArthurNovelist.com

A Note from the Author

This is the fourth edition of these three stories. They were all published previously under the general title *Barber Shop Quartet*. They are the last stories in the *Farot Quartet*.

Acknowledgments

Thanks to Morton Marcus and Don Rothman for editorial assistance. Also, thanks to Jim Mullen for the cover art and Butch Scheffler for the picture of the barber chair on the cover. And, thanks to Don Dempewolf for explaining how to determine a golfer's handicap.

Barber Shop Quartet

Barber Shop Quartet is dedicated to Mark Twain, who wrote: "All things change except barbers, the ways of barbers, and the surroundings of barbers. These never change." *From* "About Barbers"

Prologue

Before Jack-in-the-Box came to town, Belmont Shore was a quaint little Southern California coastal village, or at least that's how its inhabitants saw it. They still saw it that way even after Jack-in-the-Box. Rickety shacks on pilings, built long ago, were scattered on the beach along Ocean Boulevard. They were gradually coming down to make room for parking lots for the tourists and "flatlanders" who came to the beach on weekends and during the summer. Across the street, two and three story apartment buildings crowded one another for beach frontage. The apartments were a mixture of seasonal rentals for summer tourists and temporary homes for the year-round residents who moved into the neighborhood from such disparate places as Avon, Illinois and Obi, New York. The apartments were the dividing line between the beach cottages and the stucco and wood frame houses that lined the one-way streets streaming to and from Ocean Boulevard and Second Street.

The streets themselves were barely wide enough for parking on both sides with one lane for traffic. The parking spaces were occupied day and night by the Volkswagens of schoolteachers, the Mustangs and Rivieras of Talk-of-the-Town hustlers, the Cadillacs and Lincolns of middle-class working people, who really should have been driving Chevies and Fords but had the bigger cars because they were trying to keep up with the Joneses. There were the Alfa Romeos and Austin Healeys of playboy types who came to the Shore because they'd heard somewhere down the line that there were attractive young women everywhere and parties that lasted for days. There was indeed a grain of truth to some of that talk. As the war in Vietnam raged and college campuses across the country were rockin' 'n' rollin' between protests, the Shore, like the rest of America, was having a party.

Second Street, the main business district, was where the action was. From Quincy to Bay Shore, Second Street bustled with grocery stores and drug stores, bakeries and banks, and in this thirteen-block stretch, bars, liquor stores and real estate offices flourished on virtually every corner. There were coffee shops and pizza parlors, Mexican and Chinese restaurants, and four barber shops.

Second Street started to come alive every day at nine when the morning manager at Jack-in-the-Box started to hose down his parking lot and the adjoining sidewalk. Asa swept in front of his liquor store, and Al stood in the entryway to his jewelry store greeting early shoppers. The breakfast crowd at Sut's Hut was breaking up and going out into the morning. The air was charged with the ocean's briny aroma. Sun poured down on the avenue like drawn butter. Bernie Honig unlocked the door to his barber shop at nine on the nose.

At a time when crewcut was king and the fraternity boys were wearing Ivy League styles, Bernie's was one of the first "hairstyling" barber shops around. Campus radicalism and revolt against "the establishment" were taking hold, and long hairstyles were coming in. Bernie, knowing where the dollar was, began attending workshops and seminars to learn how to deal with the longer styles. He was ten years ahead of his time. He'd tell his customers, "I could see it coming." His appointment book was filled, and he stayed busy even after the barbers in the other shops on the avenue were playing checkers with each other in the front windows of their shops.

One And Two Halves

Bernie's shop was on a block that included a coin-operated laundry called Norge Village on one corner and a cafe on the other. Between those two businesses was a McCoy's market on one side of Bernie's shop and Asa's liquor store on the other side. The red and white plastic cylinder of his barber pole, a symbol of so many years of bloodletting and tooth pulling, revolved during business hours. A red-white-and-blue neon sign hung in the window. Its tubes were shaped to spell out the words "Bernie's Barber Shop." The vertical lines of both Bs looked like twin barber poles.

The shop had two medium-size maroon leather-upholstered iron chairs, spaced six feet apart, not huge and heavy like the old porcelain barber chairs, but also not tiny and light weight like the styling chairs that appeared later. They were smooth and cold, and they never seemed to break down or lose their luster, as though they were oblivious to the passage of time. Behind each chair were cabinets and shampoo bowls above which hung mirrors. Other mirrors were positioned on the opposite wall facing the chairs. They lined up so that when the customer in the chair was looking into either mirror, he saw his own reflection front-back, front-back until the tunnel curved upward and out of sight. A 1940s vintage cash register sat on a raised podium in the middle of a table midway between the two chairs on the opposite wall. Magazines littered the lower surface of the table, and four waiting chairs lined the wall, two on each side of the register.

Noticeable, simply by the absence of any other wall hangings, were two eight by ten black and white photographs, toward the back of the shop, of a much younger Bernie when he was an apprentice jockey in Chicago. One pictured him riding a horse to victory at Arlington Park; the other showed him on the same horse in the winner's circle, wreathed with roses.

11

Jerome Arthur

At age forty-four, Bernie was as steady and hard-working as the chair he toiled behind. His favorite expression was, "Ain't no use walk-in' around if yuh ain't makin' money." He'd walked off the ship at Terminal Island at the end of the war and gone to work at the Iowa Barber Shop in downtown Long Beach. It didn't take him long to realize that he wanted his own shop. When he bought the lease on the one in Belmont Shore, it was a one-chair operation. In the twenty years that followed, he added another chair.

Jerôme Farot, the barber in the second chair, at twenty-five, was young enough to be Bernie's son. Three months after he'd graduated from high school, he was enrolled in the barber college at Fifth and San Julian in downtown Los Angeles. He went on active duty with the Naval Reserve immediately after he passed the state board. He got lucky and got to serve his tour of duty at Los Alamitos Naval Air Station. That's how he found his way to Bernie's front door. After he got discharged early to go to Long Beach City College, he went to work afternoons and Saturdays in the second chair.

When they were both cutting hair, the shop was as busy as a beehive. Voices over-lapped, and if either of the two barbers wanted some privacy in his conversation, he'd have to lower his voice. But this was not often, as Jerôme's schedule was only half of Bernie's.

12

Bernie

I saw Clint Derrick leaning on the window sill as I rounded the corner. My first cut of the day. It was a warm morning. He was dressed in Bermuda shorts, a short sleeve crew shirt and Topsiders.

"'Mornin', Clint," I said as I got to the front door of the shop.

"Hey, Bernie."

I unlocked the door and we went in. I gave him the *Press-Telegram* I was carrying and he sat down. I turned the lights and radio on, walked to the back room, hung up my jacket and put on my apron. When I got back to my chair, I took a quick look at the schedule and saw that I was booked up all day. It was Good Friday and I figured it to be busy. Jerôme wasn't go'n'a get there till twelve-thirty, and he was booked up for the afternoon. I was go'n'a take my lunch break when he got in.

While I was in the back room, Clint had set the newspaper down on the table, gone to the cabinet next to my backbar, taken the *Playboy* out, and sat back down in the chair. I don't leave that magazine out with the others out of respect for the women and kids that come in.

"Ready for Easter?" I asked as I came out of the back room.

"Yep," he said.

He didn't usually say much during the cut, or he only spoke when I asked him a question. That was the easy part of cutting his hair. He was otherwise very particular, invariably putting me through the wringer when I was done cutting. I don't know who he thought he was, a movie star or something. His haircut had to be "perfect," according to him. If it wasn't, he'd make me take off a hair here, a hair there until he was satisfied. I suppose that was what he meant by perfect—the way *he* wanted it. It was by no means a perfect or even a good haircut as far as I was concerned.

He had naturally wavy hair that was graying a bit at the temples. It would fall right into place if he'd let it, but he was always trying to comb it in directions that it wouldn't go naturally. He was one of my first customers to use spray. He had to. Otherwise, it wouldn't lie down. His sideburns were disproportionately long for as short as his hair was, squared at the jaw line, and they were so thinned-out that they were just shadows on the sides of his face.

It wasn't enough that he had to screw up his own hair, but then he had to go and screw up his kid's hair, too. The boy was only eight or nine years old, and Clint would hover over us the whole time I was cutting the poor little guy's hair. Clint wanted the boy's haircut just like his own, and it really looked ridiculous to see a little kid who didn't even have any whiskers at all with peach fuzz sideburns about an inch long and perfectly squared. That's about as ridiculous as a bald-headed guy doing a comb-over.

Clint had a taste for expensive, unnecessary things like silk vests and brightly colored ascots. His clothes were always top-quality designer fashions, the kind of thing you saw advertised in *Playboy.*

Clint had been a regular customer every other Saturday morning for about five years. Every once in a while he'd get a Friday off, like today, and he'd schedule his haircut then. He'd only missed once about a year ago, and that was because he wanted to try the beauticians down the street at Jon Don when they first opened in Naples. He didn't believe me when I told him I'd been taking training in hairstyling, so he went down there and tried them out before he gave me a chance. He wasn't happy with the Jon Don haircut, so he came back to me. The incident motivated me to go into a total styling program sooner.

He treated everything he owned as meticulously as he did his wardrobe and grooming. He had a 'sixty-four and a half Ford Mustang parked out at the curb. It looked like it was just washed and waxed. It had all the extras: chrome rims, racing stripes, hood scoop, rear deck spoiler and cheater slicks on the rear wheels. The custom paint job was bright metallic orange, "competition orange" Clint called it. I don't know what all the car had under the hood, but I'd bet the motor was the biggest they had, and it had a four-speed floor shift. Many's the time I saw him driving down Second Street like he was racing someone, weaving in and out of traffic, speeding up, slowing down, down shifting and what have you. Mister Grand Prix.

"That's a pretty spiffy car yuh sport around in, Clint?"

"Pretty nice, huh? I'm go'n'a take it in for a tune-up, soon as I get outa' here."

"Where yuh go for that?"

"Dealer. Downtown."

"How long since your last tune-up?"

"Ten thousand. Not getting good mileage right now. That's how I noticed it before I checked the miles on the odometer. Mileage isn't all that good to begin with."

He flipped the pages of *Playboy* as he talked.

"Will yuh take a look at *that*," he says, holding up the centerfold.

I liked to keep the customer's back to the window so I could use the natural light to cut by. As Clint held up the magazine, a couple of cute little coeds passing by on the sidewalk looked in and saw all eighteen inches of Miss April in all her nudity. They just smiled and kept walking.

"Ain't that something," was about all I could say.

Then I quit cutting for a minute or so and looked over his shoulder as he turned the pages. We looked at the rest of the nudes of Miss April. When I started cutting again, I said to him,

"Did yuh see how the market did last week?"

"Didn't watch it real close. How'd it do?"

"I was watching a couple mutual funds myself. Equity and Keystone did real good. Biggest jump since I bought 'em over a year ago."

"I'm not invested in the market, myself."

That didn't surprise me, and I wasn't surprised when I found out that Clint only rented and didn't own the house he lived in on Sixty-fourth Place. Apparently, he wasn't invested in anything. I would've bet he wished he *was* invested in his own real estate, though. He had a taste for expensive things that weren't investments, like his rent, which was probably plenty high, but then nobody could own property on the Peninsula on what Clint made. I drove by his place one Sunday when I was down that way visiting another friend who lived on Seventieth Place. Clint's house looked small, probably only two bedrooms. It was a little wood frame bungalow, really no more than a vacation cottage. Just the location alone, I would've guessed it cost him about two hundred seventy-five or maybe three hundred a month.

One And Two Halves

The day I went by, his wife was watering the front yard. It was a small patch, about half the size of the front part of my barber shop. Just the right size for the woman watering it. She was only about five feet tall, but she stood a couple inches taller in her big, blond hairdo and white high heel shoes. The shoes and her white string bikini contrasted handsomely with her tanned torso, arms and legs. Odd outfit to wear for watering the lawn on Sunday morning, but she wore it well. She had a great figure.

She looked pretty much like everything else of Clint's—expensive. In a younger day she could have been a bunny at a Playboy Club, or playmate of the month like the one we'd just looked at. She was that beautiful. I suppose that suited Clint real good. He read *Playboy* every time he got his hair cut. A real "Man at his Leisure" or "What Sort of Man Reads *Playboy*?"

The mystery was where it all came from. Clint ran a rivet gun out at Douglas. He never actually told me himself he was a riveter; he always just said that he worked at Douglas. Another one of my clients later today, Stew, who's a middle management executive out there, told me that one, and I think he knew. In all the time I knew Clint and cut his hair, I never found out where he got the dough to support all his expensive tastes. Probably belonged to a good union.

"Who's go'n'a win the Derby this year, Bernie?" he suddenly asked. "Isn't it coming up pretty soon?"

"Yeah, next month. First Saturday in May. Don't know who's go'n'a win. Lota' good entries this year."

When I finished the haircut, I turned him around to face the mirror on the backbar. He got out of the chair with the haircloth still around his neck and got about a foot from

17

the mirror and examined what seemed like every hair on his head. Then he sat down and said,

"Gi'me the hand mirror."

I did and again he looked real close at it.

"Turn me around," he said.

He very meticulously examined the back of his head in the reflection of the two mirrors.

"See this?" he said pointing to a small area on the nape. "Isn't it a little crooked here?"

"Well, Clint, it just looks like that because I tried to leave it as close to the natural hairline as I could."

I explained that to him every time he got a haircut.

"Cut it off and make it straight."

And he said that to me every time. So, I cut it and that made the whole back of his head look lopsided. He looked at it again in the mirror and said,

"Perfect."

I dusted off his neck with the shampoo towel and let him out of the chair. He paid me and started out the door.

"See yuh in a couple weeks," he said as he left.

Stan hadn't arrived yet, so I cleaned up around my chair. When I finished sweeping the floor, I lit a cigarette. Stan walked in just as I was lighting up.

*   *   *

Stanley Moe was one of my best customers. He was regular, every other Friday, and he never complained about or second-guessed my work. And when his two teenage boys needed haircuts (about once a month) he'd schedule his appointment for three in the afternoon, and the boys would follow him after school. There was never any problem about how they would have their haircuts. Stan wanted them to have regular boys haircuts, and he made sure that's what they got. No argument about it. And they were polite young men to boot; they accepted what their father said when it came to their hair.

A lot of parents who brought kids in for cuts, especially the women, would let the kids dictate how they wanted their hair cut. So many times parents brought their teenage son or sons in, and it was constant arguing while I was trying to cut the hair. Doc Boyd's two were a good example of that. I thought of him right then only because I could see he was in my book for ten o'clock, twenty minutes from now. Every time he or his wife brought the kids in, they'd start hollering about how they didn't want any off the top, or how they wanted their sideburns left long, and if you even touched the part they didn't want cut, even though Doc or his wife wanted it cut, they'd raise holy hell. Then you'd spend a half hour trying to compromise so everybody'd be happy, and you'd get further and further behind schedule. More often than not I'd end up hurting somebody's feelings, and after a while I just wouldn't give a damn.

That wasn't the way it was with Stan. *He* said what kind of haircuts *his* kids got, and like their dad, they were always prepped for their cuts when they sat in my chair. Mornings like this Stan's hair was still damp from the shower, so I'd only condition it before I started cutting, but when he came in with the boys after school, I'd shampoo all three of them.

Stan was a C.P.A. and he dressed and groomed himself accordingly. He wore nice clothes and was generally a clean-cut guy. Money was not a problem for him. Getting a haircut was one of the pleasures he didn't mind paying for,

19

and he'd leave me a buck tip every time. In fact, he enjoyed it so much that every once in a while, he'd stop in on his way home from work and get a shampoo and blow dry just for the sheer pleasure of it. Nothing but the best for Stan. He drove a new Mercedes Benz and had a Cal Twenty in a slip at the Marina. He got a therapeutic massage twice a month, and once a week he took his wife out to dinner and drinks. He was truly a gentleman with a lot of class.

"You and the missus going out to dinner tonight?" I asked.

"Oh, yeah. Every Friday. Goin' down to Seal Beach to the Glide'r Inn."

"Slummin' it, huh?"

"Hey, Glide'r Inn's a nice place. Food's good and the price is right. Don't feel like I got'a spend a bundle every time we go out."

"Stan, I'd rather have your dough than a license to steal."

"Any money I've got, I've worked my tail off for, and it didn't come easy. That's the problem with this younger generation. They want it all handed to 'em on a silver platter. They don't seem to realize that you've got'a work if you want nice things. A lot of 'em just wan'a drop out and do nothing. Not all of 'em mind you."

"Seems that's true, huh?"

"Absolutely."

"Real good example of one a' the hard workin' ones is the guy owns the bar across the street," I said, swiveling the chair so Stan could see.

"You mean the Acapulco Inn?" he said.

"Yup. He was smart with his money at a real young age. He bought some real estate in Seal Beach. I think he owns three houses down there, one in Old Town and two in that new housing tract across the highway. Took the money he got in rent and rolled it over into the market. Just bought the bar couple months ago. Real gold mine. The fella' delivers his beer gets his haircut from me, and he says that little bar sells more Coors than any other bar in Long Beach. Jerôme's a regular over there, and he knows the guy. Cuts his hair. Says he don't work a regular job."

"How'd he get his start?" Stan asked.

"I don't know for sure. Probably had a day job to begin with. 'Fact, I think he started out workin' at Douglas. Might've inherited some money somewhere along the line. He's only about thirty; couldn't't've made all of it workin'. 'Sides, he's not the workin' type. Hates to work in his own damn bar. Says he don't like dealing with drunks. About the only time he goes over there is to collect the money. I guess he'll have a few beers time to time. Got it made."

"He have any kind of overhead?"

"Certainly. Everybody in business has overhead and expenses," I said, "but what the hell could his overhead be? Bar's not much bigger'n Asa's liquor store and he pays his help the minimum wage. Now, I ain't no accountant or mathematician, but I c'n see he's got low overhead. Plus, he's got bowlin' machines, pool tables and pinball machines. Can't hardly ever get a game of pool 'cause there's so many people waitin' in line. I'd bet one bowlin' machine pays his rent. You've got'a figure his pool money and beer money are prit'near clear profit. He's got a good deal over there. So good, he's talkin' about opening another joint down the street."

I'd been topping Stan's hair the whole time I was talking. When I finished that, I towel-dried the sides and back. It was then we quit talking for a while, and he opened the same *Playboy* Clint had been looking at. I picked up my seven-inch shears and worked on the taper on the sides and back.

"Besides having it made money-wise," I broke the silence, "he does all right with the gals, too. He drives a swell new El Camino Chevrolet and has a sailboat in the Marina. Like you. Hey, maybe you've seen 'im on the water. His boat's a Columbia Twenty-two. He's got a Volkswagen sand buggy, too. Yellow."

"You know, I think his slip's somewhere around the same basin I'm in. I've seen that car in the Marina parking lot, and I've actually seen him a couple times powering out the channel to the outside."

"He have some knock-out looking gals with him?"

"You know, I believe he did."

"I hear he's a real ladies' man."

I put up my shears and began to clean up the nape of his neck with my Wahls when Sam Lighters stuck his head in the door and said,

"Hey, Jackson, can I still get a number in the pool?"

Sam called everybody "Jackson."

"Sam, I haven't had a pool on the feature race in months. You know that."

"I know, but I still wanted to check with you in case you changed your mind and started doing it again."

He turned and went into the liquor store. He used to be Asa's partner, but he sold his interest a couple years before, and he still came down and hung around behind the counter with Asa. Sam was actually the original owner and Asa bought in later.

One And Two Halves

I was doing the fin- ishing touches on Stan's haircut. When I was done, I tried to give him the hand mirror so he could see the completed job up close, but he said it was okay and handed the mirror right back to me without even looking at the cut. I undid the haircloth, trimmed the hair at the base of his neck, and wiped his nape with some Jeris talc on the dry part of the shampoo towel. Then I combed his hair into place and shot it with a light mist of hairspray. He paid me for the haircut and, as usual, left me a buck tip.

"Thanks a lot, Stan" I said. "Have a nice Easter."

"You too, Bernie. See yuh in a couple weeks."

Then he left.

*   *   *

I was keeping right on schedule. Doc Boyd hadn't come in yet, so I had a chance to light up another cigarette and sweep the floor again. Just then the phone rang.

"Hi." It was Trisha's slow, sexy voice. "I was just thinking about you, so I decided to call and see what you were doing."

"N...nothing," I stammered. "Having a smoke and waiting for my next customer. How're *you*? Sound like you just woke up."

"I'm still in bed and feeling kinda' lonely." Trisha was a cocktail waitress at Hoefly's who lived in the Whispering Sands apartments down on Ocean. Her shift was five to midnight, Wednesday through Saturday. "Think you could come over during your lunch break. I've got something for you."

"Can't today. Booked solid. Only got a half hour for lunch."

Jerome Arthur

I looked out the window and saw Doc Boyd crossing the street coming in my direction.

"Listen, my next customer just came in," I said, keeping my voice down. "Call me next week. It'll be slow after the holiday. Looks like I got some time Tuesday afternoon, your day off."

"I don't know if I can wait that long," she said, her sexy voice flowing into my ear and making me horny as hell. "But I guess I don't have any choice, do I?"

"Believe me, I wish I could get over there today, but I can't. Listen, kid, I got'a go, okay? Talk to you next week."

My boxer shorts felt damp, and I was throbbing, but there was nothing I could do about it. Good thing I'm wearing an apron.

"Okay," she sighed, sounding pouty and coquettish all at the same time. "I'll talk to you next week then, but I'll have to find somebody to take care of me in the meantime. Bye."

She hung up.

When I turned back to my chair, I was looking at Doc's completely bald head. He was balder'n me. At least I had a couple strands going across the top of my head. He'd picked up the *Playboy* before he sat down and was looking at the centerfold.

Doc Boyd looked more like a trucker or plumber than a doctor. He had a potbelly on a heavy-set frame and a ruddy complexion. You knew by his delicate hands and his educated vocabulary that he wasn't a tradesman. He wore a conservative suit and tie on weekdays when he went into the office, but on weekends, which started Friday, he dressed casually. That Friday he wore khakis and a sport shirt. He and his wife were conserva- tive Republicans, both active members of the John Birch Society.

"So, what's new, Doc?"

"Not much. How about you?"

"Same ol' sixes and sevens."

"You see the story in this morning's *Press-Telegram* about this socialized medicine program Johnson signed into law last year? Between that and all this civil rights nonsense, we won't have any freedom left at all by the time he's done. The next thing you know, we'll have to get the government's permission to go to the bathroom."

"You're fired up today, huh, Doc?"

"I'm just afraid of what this country is coming to. If socialized medicine is what they want, I'm the guy who can give it to 'em. When I was in the Army in the war, I used to see as many as fifty patients a day, so I know what it's like when a medical practice becomes an assembly line. If they want me to do it again, I'll do it. I'm not proud, but if they take the money incentive out of it, I'll see the fewest patients as I possibly can. Why work harder for less money? What would you do, Bernie, if the government told you how much money you could make?"

"I agree with you, Doc, but the question is what can we do about it?" I knew damn well he was seeing patients every ten minutes and charging a minimum of twenty-five bucks a pop, not counting medication. "You know, Cronkite says Johnson got a mandate from the people. Don't you think he knows what the people in this country want?"

"If you're talking about Cronkite, he's just a part of the Communist conspiracy. If you're talking about Johnson, then I say what about the twenty-five million or so of us who voted for Goldwater? Do we, as a minority, have to relin-

25

quish our liberty to the majority? Johnson got elected fairly and squarely, and in no way do I fault him for that, but I think he's usurping too much power and using it to legislate us into a classless society. He's taking away from me what I worked hard for, and giving it to somebody else who didn't do anything. Let them get a job like I did and earn it the way I did. I worked hard for what I've got. Why should I be penalized just because I have it? Why should somebody else get something they didn't work for? It just burns my *ass*."

"I agree with you a hundred percent, Doc. It's the same story with this barber shop. I've worked here for twenty years making a living, building a business, and then they come along with one Negro and make me cut his hair whether I want to or not, and that's the end of my business. So, you think any of my regular customers would ever come back if they saw me cutting a Negro's hair?" I found myself whispering.

"Know exactly what you mean. Medicare? It'll benefit Negroes mostly. Why should they get free medical care while whites have to pay for it? That's discrimination.

"Vietnam War's the only thing Johnson's doing right, and he's botching that job, too. We must hold the Communists in check. We can't be pussy footing around. Since when can't the United States of America, the most powerful nation in the world with the best government in the history of western civilization, beat a backward little country like North Vietnam? We ought to go in there and bomb the hell out of 'em. We could wipe Vietnam off the map with one bomb. I think Ronald Reagan's got the right idea when he says we ought'a make a parking lot out of the country. How long we been foolin' around over there? Four years? Five years? It's been almost two years since Johnson got the

Tonkin Resolution through Congress. What the hell's he waiting for? Why doesn't he let the generals win it? If we lose that war, we lose all of Asia, and then our days *will* be numbered. Once Asia is lost, it's just a matter of time before we lose the rest of the world. Then we'll have Russians and Chinese pulling into Alamitos Bay. You can bet your life on that."

"Talkin' about the domino theory, right?"

"I most certainly am," he replied. "I've read quite a bit about it. If Truman had let MacArthur go into Manchuria when we were in Korea instead of firing him, we might not have some of the troubles we're having today.

"It started long before the Korean war, though. Roosevelt sold out to the Communists at Yalta. From there they've fallen like dominoes, one by one. We gave half of Europe away to the Russians at the end of the war. Then in '56 we left the Hungarians to suffer under the iron hand of Communism. Three years after Hungary, we gave 'em Cuba. Now the question is who's next? I think it's South Vietnam, unless we stay the course."

Since Doc Boyd didn't have much hair to work with, I was practically finished cutting it. Even though I wanted to keep on talking to him (it certainly was an interesting discussion), I couldn't, because my next customer, Clay Doyle, had just come into the shop. He went straight to the door to the back room and to the restroom.

"Only time will tell," I said, trying to wind up the conversation. As I dusted Doc's neck off, he echoed me,

"Only time will tell. I just hope we can make it for a few more years. Maybe then my boys'll have a chance to get some of the good out of life that I've been able to get. Speaking of which, can my wife bring the boys in next Tues-

27

day after school? You got a couple of openings in your schedule?"

"Well, how about Wednesday," I said, remembering I wanted to keep Tuesday afternoon open for Trisha.

"Oh, sure. That'll be fine."

As he got out of the chair, I turned to look at the appointment book.

"What time they get out?"

"Three o'clock, so both of 'em can be here by three-thirty. Can you do 'em then?"

"Certainly."

I filled out a card with the date and time of the appointments and gave it to him. He paid me and gave me a half-buck tip.

"Thanks, Doc. Have a nice Easter."

By the time I got the words out, he was already out the door and on his way down the street.

*   *   *

Clay hadn't come out of the restroom yet, so I went back that way to get the broom. I swept the floor, and as I was emptying the dustpan into the trash can next to the restroom, Clay came out. We walked together up to the chair.

"How's it goin', Clay?" I said as we walked back out to the chair.

"Pretty good," he replied. "Been to Europe since the last time I saw you."

"Really? Where 'bout?"

"Florence, Italy."

"It's only been two weeks since your last cut."

One And Two Halves

"Left day after I was in. Just got home Wednesday night. Only stayed in Florence. Didn't go anywhere else. Great trip. You should see some of the art in that town. Italian Renaissance started there."

I toweled the excess water from his hair and raised the chair upright.

"Ever travel to the Orient?" I asked.

"Never have. I'm leery about going to places like that. Worry about our safety, and yuh just get beat down by the end of the trip, from the poverty, dirty streets, all that. People always beggin' for money, and yuh know, by the end of it you're just tired. 'Sides, where you go'n'a travel over there? 'Bout the only places you can go are Japan and Taiwan. Big upheaval in Red China right now; government won't let you go there anyway; and war's goin' on in Vietnam. Thailand and South Korea might not be too bad, but we just don't wan'a go there. Europe's the place."

I was working right along on his haircut. I got the outline in over the ears, and I'd just finished topping it.

"So, besides the trip, what else you been up to?"

"Tryin' to sell some books, and I'm getting ready to sell my house, too."

Clay had a small rare-books business he ran out of his house.

"Really? You movin'?"

"Yeah."

"What yuh go'n'a do with the books?"

"Take 'em with me."

"Where yuh go'n'a move to. Go'n'a move in with Lois?"

"Don't think I wan'a move into *her* house, but we may get another house together."

29

"You guys go'n'a buy a house?"

"Yeah. We have to. Her house is too big. Kinda' like to get something a little smaller."

"You got a pretty big house yourself, right?"

"Big house, no yard. We're looking for something smaller. Maybe Old Town Seal Beach."

"Don't wan'a look at anything in the Shore?"

"Nah. Seems like it's more crowded here than Seal Beach. Probably not, but it seems like it."

"How much you askin' for your place."

"Lot more'n I thought at first."

"Oh, really?"

"Still tryin' to work out the timing, and my kids ought'a be involved in whatever decision I make."

"Absolutely."

His two girls were both in college. One was still living at home and going to State; the other one was up in Santa Barbara going to U.C. Clay's wife died of cancer a few years ago.

"I'm tryin' to figure out what I need to do as far as remodeling. I've got'a get the floors refinished...floor guy, plaster guy...fix it up...make it look acceptable. Needs some work anyway."

"Yeah, but *now* you're tryin' to sell it."

"When I've got different agents who've got good reputations, and who I respect, all telling me the same stuff without talking to each other, I got'a think they know what the hell they're talking about."

"Absolutely."

I was using my Osters to taper up the neckline and sideburns.

One And Two Halves

"Lois went out to U.C. Irvine the other day. She applied to their M.F.A. program."

"Where?"

"The new U.C. out in Irvine. Just opened last September."

"What's M.F.A. stand for?"

"Master of Fine Arts. Her area's Photography."

"Oh, really? She go in for that kinda' thing?"

"Yeah, thinks she wants to teach. She has two degrees, but neither one of 'em's in photography."

"Uh, huh. The M.F.A., that's a writing degree, too. Right?"

"It can be. It's pretty much the terminal degree for lots of stuff."

"And hers is for photography? That sounds real swell."

"They only take five or six people in photography, and over a hundred applied," Clay said.

"Wow!"

"Somewhat competitive."

"*I guess*," I said.

"They didn't have one at Long Beach when I was going there, yuh know? Still don't. They just have a straight M.A. program."

"Right, right."

"They've got all kind of odd ball programs in college these days. I heard of one that's so popular nobody can get in. It's a graduate program in wine marketing."

"Wow! Where they got that one?"

"U.C. Davis. It's turned out to be a big deal there."

"Is that right? Davis's got a wine marketing…?"

"Davis is the *best* program for wine marketing," he said before I could finish my question. "They call it wine marketing, but it's really a vintner's school. Davis's an interesting school. Got a lota' different programs there. Big ag. school. Sports teams're called the Aggies? I'm sure that's how the wine marketing fits in. Also, their veterinary school. They got a good one of those, and I hear they just started a medical school."

"Okay. We're go'n'a block this back here, right?"

"Yeah."

Clay had short hair and really shouldn't have blocked the neckline, but that's what he wanted, so that's what I gave 'im.

"I'm getting what my ophthalmologist calls an ocular migraine right now," I said. "There's no pain. It's just I got this little thing in my right eye, and he said...he used the word crenellated? You know what crenellated is?"

"Roof line of a castle."

"Yeah. That's what this looks like. It's like a gear."

"It's got those little bumps?"

"Yeah. It's just my right eye, and it goes away...ten, fifteen minutes, and there's no pain."

"You know what it is."

"Yeah. Just looks strange. One happened a couple a' days before my ophthalmologist came in for his haircut. You know Kenneth Trager? When I told him my symptoms, he told me what it was and that it would go away in a few minutes, and it did. It scared me when it first happened, but now I'm kinda' used to it. He said there's no-thin' you can do about it. Just wait and it goes away."

"He say what causes it or anything?"

32

One And Two Halves

"Nah. Maybe, but I can't remember what it was. Hell, I can't even remember what I did an hour ago. He might've said what caused it," I chuckled.

I was finished with the haircut, so I turned him to the mirror, and he said,

"Looks good, Bern."

I pulled the haircloth off of him, and as he got out of the chair, I turned and looked at my schedule, and went forward to Friday two weeks out. I wrote his name in at three o'clock. I copied his phone number from the present day. Then I got my card out and wrote the appointment on the back.

"There yuh go, Clay. See yuh in two weeks."

*   *   *

It was go'n'a be an hour and a half before Jerôme'd get in to relieve me for lunch. I'd just lit a cigarette when a blond kid with mutton chop sideburns and a bushy mustache stepped into the doorway and asked,

"You trim mustaches and sideburns?"

"Yeah, I do, but I'm all booked up today. Still got one opening tomorrow, if you're interested," I said, as I turned to look at the appointment book. Jerôme's afternoon was full up, too.

"Kinda' wanted to get it done today," and before I had a chance to give him a card, he was out the door and on his way down the street.

I took a couple drags off my cigarette when I saw Drew crossing the street heading toward the shop. I put the cigarette out and dumped the ashtray into the bin in my backbar. Drew sat down in the chair.

"Mornin', Drew. How're yuh doin' today?"

"Fine, thanks. How 'bout yourself?"

"Busy. I'm booked today. Hardly find time for a smoke."

"Can't complain if you're busy, right?"

"Right."

Drew was big, about six-two or -three, and heavyset. His hair was graying and he had a rough, course complexion. His face was badly pockmarked, and it looked like the pits had dirt ground into them. He wasn't dirty. He just looked dirty, and that was inconsistent with the rest of his appearance. If you were to see him on the street wearing overalls and coaxing a jackhammer, you wouldn't give it a second thought, but this guy was a classy dresser. He was like Stan in that respect, and just as you could tell that Stan was a professional, you could tell Drew was, too.

He showed his education when he talked. He was an A.C.L.U. lawyer. I couldn't figure why he worked for them when I knew he could make more dough working for a private outfit. Then one time we started talking politics. He was just the opposite of Doc Boyd, an extreme liberal, favoring things like socialized medicine and civil rights. That part of it didn't make sense to me. He was about the same age as I was, and I know he went through the same Depression I went through. He claimed it was the Depression that formed his political philosophy.

"Seeing all that suffering just made me want to help those who couldn't help themselves," he'd once said. "What the American Civil Liberties Union's all about. Helping the downtrodden."

I didn't agree with him at all on that one, but that was how he felt, so I didn't say anything. I think with a little initiative and ambition, you can be as rich or poor as you want.

"How we go'n'a cut your hair today?" I asked after he was settled in the chair and the haircloth was fastened around his neck.

"The usual," he said with a slight smile and a quick, almost unnoticeable wink of his left eye. "Make it special, huh? For Easter."

His thick gray hair was real easy to cut. He parted it on the left, and it laid naturally over to one side with a slight wave in front. He had a nice, even, medium taper, and his sideburns were smooth and tapered to match the neckline.

"What're yuh doin' for the holiday?" I asked, as I raised his clean, conditioned head out of the sink.

"Having dinner at home with the family. If the weather's anything like it is today, we might all go down to the beach for a while. How about you? What're you doing?"

"Probably spend a quiet day with the family. Folks'll be coming over. I can't afford to do much of anything else, as much as I'd like to."

"Oh come on, Bernie," he said agreeably. "You can't be playing it that close to the ground."

"Well, I wouldn't go so far as to say that. Uncle Sam gets through with me, not much left. Better off on welfare. That's what's happening, you know. People can make more on welfare than they can working, so they're milkin' the government for every dime they can get. And, yuh know, that's us."

"Now, you know that's not true. I'm sure there are people who are taking advantage of the system, but most of the people who get welfare or unemployment are truly in need. What's a single woman with kids supposed to do? She

35

can't go out and get a job because there's nobody to take care of her kids. Or what about the guy who can't find a job? How's he feed his family? These people have got to be provided for. Sure, your taxes are high, and some of it is lost to welfare fraud, but for the most part those welfare programs help a lot of needy people. Besides, look at the services you get in return for the taxes you pay."

"What services do I get for my money?" I hoped my sarcasm was showing.

"Well, you have a pretty good retirement program with Social Security," he said.

"If I live that long! Let's say I become a millionaire and can't draw it. Will I get the money back that I put into it? I bet I don't."

"That's not true. If you contribute to the system, you get to draw on it, and it's a good system for the majority of Americans. And now President Johnson has gotten the congress to pass a health care program for seniors. When you get old, you'll be glad you have it. Now we need to get a health care program for the rest of us, something doesn't require us to get insurance from private companies."

"I agree with Ronald Reagan when he says that some people make a profession out of collecting welfare. It's about time these people started showing some ambition and initiative and started pulling their own weight."

My outburst surprised me, as I didn't usually say things like that to Drew. His right eyebrow shot up when I mentioned Reagan's name, and the pleasant smile disappeared from his face. It was one of those rare moments when Drew showed his bad temper.

"That insensitive son-of-a-bitch!" he said. "It'll be just our luck that he'll get elected governor, too."

36

One And Two Halves

That was the last thing Drew said to me that day, except "goodbye" when he left, and I thought it would be the last time I'd ever see him, but it wasn't. He must've really liked my haircuts.

I started blowing his hair dry when Mort Soames came in. Mort went straight to the *Playboy* in the cabinet next to my backbar. When Drew's hair was dried, I combed it into place, and it was looking real nice. Like I said before, it was a perfect head of hair. I dusted off the back of his neck and loosened up the haircloth. I took my four-aught blade and trimmed the hair from the base of his neck. Then I dusted off the back of his neck with the shampoo towel.

When I saw his face in the round hand mirror, it had that cheerful look on it again, any trace of hostility gone from it. He nodded his approval and got out of the chair reaching for his wallet. He paid and tipped me a buck without further comment, smiled and said goodbye, disappearing out the front door into the crowd of bikinis and cutoff blue jeans and bare feet.

*   *   *

"Okay, Mort," I said. "You ready?"

"Sure," he said, closing the *Playboy* and stepping into the chair. "Looks like the mayor's got a quorum over there."

He raised his chin in the direction of the four old men gathered at the bus stop bench across the street. They were regulars on that corner most weekdays. Two of them had canes propped between their knees, palms resting on the handles. They all wore hearing aids and different styles of Panama hats (one fedora, two plantations and one stingy

37

brim). The one Mort called the mayor, the one wearing the fedora, was pacing back and forth lecturing the other three sitting on the bench. Everybody called him the Mayor of Second Street.

"They hang around over there a lot," I said. "Sidewalk supervisors when the city resurfaced Second Street last year."

Mort was a frustrated businessman who taught business administration up at State College, a perfect example of the old saying, "Those who can, do; those who can't, teach." He was a real fancy dresser, and he had a good line, but for one reason or another, he never made a go of it in any business he ever tried. As a teacher he must've had some good advice because businessmen were calling on him for counsel all the time.

"Went on another trip since the last time I saw you," he said as I was shampooing his hair.

"Oh? Where to this time?"

"Boise, Idaho."

"What were you doing there?"

"Frienda' mine is opening a new territory for his electronics business. Went up to interview a prospective district manager."

"How'd it go?"

"Great! Had a ball. You won't believe what happened. I didn't think it'd be much when we landed. From the air, it was the wide-open spaces, mountains to the north and a couple lazy rivers tumbling down. As we came down to the runway, I saw a rooftop sign rush beneath us that said, "Boise Municipal Airport," and, if you can believe it, a windsock. Air was so clear I couldn't believe it. First thing I thought was I couldn't wait to get back home so I could tell the fella's on campus about it. Thinking I wouldn't have much to tell."

"Pretty small town, small airport, eh?"

"I'll say. Bill'd been there before, and he said that the town wasn't what it looked like at first glance. He'd booked us rooms at a place called the Boise Hotel. Can't get much more small town than that. Ol' Bill gets all excited soon's we get off the plane. Rubbing his hands together and inhaling the fresh air. Says something like, 'This town's loaded with action.' I was skeptical."

Mort was really on a roll. I couldn't get a word in edgewise so I just let him go and kept working on his hair.

"Got our rooms and rested up a little before dinner. At supper, Bill and I went over our plans for the next day, setting up our questions and proposals for our man. Bill had already made arrangements as to where and when we'd meet him. We smoked and talked over an apéritif. Then we went out to find the 'action.' We went to a bar Bill'd been to before. I was game for anything. I'd never been to Boise.

"As we got out of the cab at the bar, I heard a piano playing from within over voices and the clinking of ice cubes in glasses. The monotone of murmuring voices was only broken occasionally by a woman's shrill laughter and the raucous guffaw of some howling drunk. We walked in and were literally surrounded by bar noise in the dim light. After our eyes adjusted, Bill poked me. Told me to take a look at a couple a' dolls in a booth in the corner. I craned my head toward where he was pointing, and by the time I looked back at him, he was already on his way over there."

"No foolin' around, huh?"

"Not for him. He walked right over to their booth, asked if we could join them and offered 'em a drink?"

Jerome Arthur

I was halfway through the haircut by now.

"The ladies obviously weren't shy. I kept my place by the door so I couldn't hear what they were talking about, but they must've told Bill to join 'em, 'cause he turned and waved me over. After the introductions Bill sat down next to the brunette, and I sat next to the blond. Her name was Barb, and the brunette was Mary. Both real lookers. We chatted 'em up through another round, and then we took 'em back to our hotel. Once I got her in the sack, she turned me every which way but loose. Next day Bill told me he got the same action with Mary.

"In the mornin' Bill and I had breakfast at a greasy spoon around the corner from our hotel. Our appointment with his prospective district manager was a lunch date, so I spent the time after breakfast getting packed and ready to go. Met Bill at about eleven o'clock, and we went over our notes and made sure we had all of our questions in order. Then we went to the restaurant and waited for our man to show. He came and introduced himself, and we talked through lunch. He was a pretty impressive guy; he had all the right answers to our questions, and he even had some ideas of his own. Bill hired him on the spot, and as a courtesy he invited us to have dinner with him and his wife that night.

"We hadn't planned to spend another night in town, but since the previous night had been so much fun, and Bill wanted to see this guy in action, we accepted his invitation and stayed over another night. Bill and I got together again at about six o'clock and went to the restaurant where we had a martini at the bar.

"Bill's man arrived with his wife at seven, and get this for a surprise ending. I almost croaked when they came into the restaurant. His wife was Barb, the gal I'd screwed the night before. I couldn't believe it, but the lady was so cool that she carried it off as if we'd never met."

"Wow," I said. "How did *you* act?"

"I stammered at first, but after I got my composure, everything was okay. We had a very pleasant dinner together, and Barb's husband didn't seem to suspect anything. When it was over, they went their way and we went ours. We caught our plane the next morning. It was one hell of a trip."

"'Sounds like it," I said. "How do you swing these trips, anyway?"

"No problem for me. Don't pay a thing. Like this trip. Bill paid for everything, and he'll use it as a tax write-off. It's a business expense."

"Must be nice."

"It is," he said quickly, "but I've had it not-so-good, too, so I'm just now collecting for all the bad times in the past. Teaching college is really a breeze. I've got it made."

Just then I looked out the window and saw Jerôme locking his bike up to the parking meter in front of the Acapulco Inn.

"So, does that mean your classes aren't affected by the Vietnam protests, then?"

"Not yet, but it prob'ly won't be long. Students are getting restless. I'm lucky 'cause mine are pretty conservative, so they probably won't be as hard to deal with as the poli. sci. majors. Quite frankly, I don't care what they do, as long as they keep it out of my classroom. I try to be as easy to get along with as possible. When the lid blows off up there, some people will really be in bad shape, and if they'd use their heads, they could prevent it before it starts."

"Wha'da yuh mean...?" and before I could finish, he said,

"Why academic freedom, of course. There isn't much of it at State, especially for the students. You can't express yourself openly and candidly without being reprimanded by somebody. Look what happened to that graduate art student who tried to have a showing of his master's thesis on campus. The president declared it obscene and refused to allow him to show it."

"Was it obscene?"

"That's not the point. It's his expression of himself. It's his statement. He's communicating an idea. For all we know, it's an infringement on his First Amendment right of free speech. At the very least, it's censorship."

"Well, I hope when the lid blows off, it doesn't mess things up as bad as it did at Berkeley."

"It won't get that bad here. State is much more conservative than Cal," he said, stepping out of the chair, "but you mark my words, something's go'n'a happen. How much I owe yuh, Bernie?"

"Five bucks."

He took a ten out of his wallet, gave it to me and asked for four singles for change.

"Thanks a lot, Mort."

"Have a nice Easter," he said. "See yuh in a couple weeks."

"Okay."

*   *   *

He turned and went out the door. I walked over to the register and put the money in. As I straightened things up around my chair, Larry Boss- ier stuck his head in and asked me if I was ready. I told him I was, and he turned, as he usually did, and went into Asa's. A minute later he was back with a sixteen-ounce can of Hamms. He sat down in the chair, popped it open and flipped the pop-top into the hair on the floor. I got the broom and swept the floor. When I got back to the chair, he was sipping his beer and looking at the financial section of the newspaper.

"Say, Bernie, how 'bout this Keystone Fund?" he said, as I wrapped him up for his haircut. "I could've bought it low last month, but I didn't and I'm sorry now."

"No kiddin'," I said.

He was always saying, "I could've" done this or that, but as far as I could figure out, he never did the things he said he could've done, so I always thought he was only *talking*.

"Say, Bernie, look here. I.B.M. closed at two thirty-six and three quarters. Yuh know, I could've bought shares when it was only two and a quarter."

"Yeah," I said, thinking again that he was only *talking* some good finances. Asa came in and said,

"You know, Larry, they really did run wild the other night."

"I'll say they did, and what did they gain by it?" Larry said.

"I guess they'll get ahead one way or the other."

Asa no sooner got the words out of his mouth than a customer walked into his store, so he left and Larry never got to answer him. I never could figure out what those two were talking about. Asa usually started with some cryptic remark, and Larry replied with one equally obscure. Then Asa would get one last lick in and go back into his store. Af-

43

ter a couple minutes of thought, Larry would follow Asa into the liquor store and, I guess, continue the abstract discussion.

The phone rang. It was a prospective new customer wanting to get in that day. I looked at the appointment book and told him that the earliest opening either of us had was the next day. He said he couldn't wait till then.

After I hung up, I turned back to my chair, but Larry was gone. His half-empty beer can sat on the arm of the chair, and the financial section was scrunched up on the seat. Clippings of his hair left a trail from the front of the chair out the door and around the corner into the liquor store. I was always cleaning up after him. I couldn't figure that bastard out. An elementary school principal and as irresponsible as a skid row wino! It just didn't make any sense.

I stuck my head into the liquor store and told him to get back into the chair. He kept screwing around talking to Asa as I waited. It was bad enough that he'd make his appointments just before I went to lunch, but then here he was yakking with Asa in the middle of the haircut. If he didn't get back in the shop pretty soon, he was *really* go'n'a cut into my lunch break. He was an easy haircut so it wasn't go'n'a be too bad. He finally came back, the haircloth draped around him and hair clippings falling all over the place. He got back in the chair.

"Larry," I said, "how'd you ever get into school teaching? I mean, I'd think with your expertise, you could make your living in the stock market."

I tried to keep the sarcasm out of my voice. After all, I'd heard the story more than once.

"You overestimate my talents, my friend." He took himself way too seriously. "Indeed, I'd like to play the Market for a living, but education is more secure."

44

One And Two Halves

"Why'd yuh go the way yuh did?"

"I had my master's degree when I went in the Army during the war, so when I got out, I thought I'd try to get a job teaching junior college. In addition, my wife and I decided that we wanted to live out in the country, so the plan was to try the J.C.s in Orange County first. If I could get a job out there, we could buy a house somewhere nearby. Those days that was the sticks."

"How come you wound up principal in elementary school?"

"In those days you had to have some high school experience to teach junior college. Today I think it's easier to get a J.C. job without experience. 'Fact, the less you have, the better, 'cause you're cheaper than an experienced teacher. They also wan'a get rid of the image that junior colleges are just glorified high schools, so they're not necessarily hiring from the high school ranks anymore.

"It was already September and time was running out. If I was go'n'a get a teaching job, it'd better be soon. So, I decided I'd try for a lower level, and I went out to the district office of Long Beach City Schools.

"When I inquired there, they had one third grade opening right over here at Lowell, so I talked to the principal, and he offered me a contract. I signed it, and quick too. That's how I got started. I got to liking elementary education, so I stayed at Lowell and taught a few years until the principalship opened up, and when they offered it to me, I took it. I used my G.I. bill and bought the house where we still live in Belmont Heights. The wife and I raised our kids in that house. So much for moving out to the country."

He was holding his empty Hamms can and crinkling it with his fingers. I was drying his hair and beginning to feel hunger pangs. I looked out the front window and saw Jerôme unlocking his bike and walking it across the street. His first customer of the day, Hutch, was with him. A couple minutes later he was locking the bike to the meter right outside my front window.

"Wha'da yuh thinka' Shoemaker winning four races the other day?" Larry said. I welcomed the change of subject. "Do yuh think he'll win this year's Derby?"

"Sure can ride, can't he?" I said. "You know, I hear he's a real jerk. I got a customer works in valet parking out at the track, says Shoemaker never tips him, but a guy like Arcaro is a real good tipper."

"No kiddin'. So, the Shoe's a cheap skate, huh?"

"That's what I hear. Yuh know, these jockeys nowadays got it made. They have drugs and diet pills to keep their weight down. I's riding, only way to do light was to watch what yuh ate. I'd have a salad with vinegar and oil for lunch and a glass of water for dinner, and on top a' that, it was exercise, exercise, exercise."

"No kiddin'."

That's all he said, which surprised me. I thought sure he'd start pounding my ear about horse racing the way he pounded it about the Market.

"Hey, Bernie," Jerôme said as he entered the shop.

"Hey, Jerôme, how's it goin'?" I said.

I took a moment to call the delicatessen next door to the liquor store and order my lunch. Since I only had a half-hour before my next cut, it would speed things up, and my food would be ready when I got there.

I finished cutting Larry's hair and dusted off the back of his neck with the shampoo towel. After I let him look at the neckline, I took the haircloth off, and he stepped

One And Two Halves

out of the chair. He paid me and left. When I turned from the register back to my chair, I saw the empty Hamms can bent in half on top of my tools on the backbar. I cleaned up the mess and got the hell out of there, leaving Jerôme towel-drying Hutch's hair.

Jerôme

As I kick my leg over the rear wheel of my bike, dismounting in front of the A.I., I can hear the jukebox sound of "Rainy Day Women 12 & 35," drifting out the open front door. It's about five after twelve on Good Friday, and I've just come from the library up at State. I studied there for about forty-five minutes after my ten o'clock class. Now it's on to Bernie's to cut some hair this afternoon. Lunch first at the A.I.

I lock my bike to the parking meter directly in front of the bar door. As I enter, the music gets louder, but not unbearable. Mike Corvette is tending bar, and he wouldn't have it too loud. Not his style. His real name is Mike Burgess; he got the nickname because he still drives a cherry '53 Chevy Corvette that he bought new. There are about five people at the bar hunched over icy mugs. Mike is moving up and down, stocking the coolers and glass racks. Someone calls out my name,

"Hey Jerôme, what's happening? You're not supposed to be here. You're supposed to be across the street cuttin' hair."

The voice sounds familiar, but I'm not sure I know who it is right away, because I can't see much in the dark, smoky atmosphere, but as I move down the bar, I'm starting to make out Hutch's blond hair and red moustache. He's my first appointment a half hour from now, and sitting next to him is Sixto Del Toro, who follows him at one o'clock. A half-empty pitcher of beer sits on the bar between them.

One And Two Halves

"Pool up a stool," Sixto says. He's got a heavy Mexicano accent.

"Give 'im a glass," Hutch says to Corvette.

Mike sets the glass on the bar, and I order a Special. While he's fixing it, Sixto pours me a beer from the pitcher, and I sip. It hits the spot.

When the last lines from the Dylan tune play out, I say,

"Man, that guy's good."

"Yeah," Hutch says, "and he writes his own material, too."

"I'm hip. And yuh know, that's the best part of his act, the lyrics."

"Don't know if it's the *best* part, but it's definitely *one* of the best parts. Since he went electric, the music's gotten a lot better, too."

After being in the bar for a few minutes, I adjust to the darkness and things come into focus. The other three people at the bar are alone. Their blank stares glaze over the posters of bullfighters and pictures and other assorted junk on the wall behind the bar. One of the posters has a picture of some tropical beach paradise, and it says simply, "Jamaica?" And written under the question is someone's graffiti, "No, but I tried."

The A.I. allows anybody and everybody to bring anything in to put up behind the bar. The false ceiling is a parachute that billows down over the bar. In the back there are two coin-operated pool tables. There used to be a ping-pong table back there, too, but Lon, the last owner of the place, got rid of it and replaced it with the more lucrative pool tables. There're a couple college guys with a pitcher playing eight ball.

Tonight and tomorrow will be big nights for them and hundreds of others like them. The apartments and cottages along the beach will be bulging with them and other teeny-boppers and bubble gummers from up in Los Angeles and the flatlands. Easter week at the beach is party time for them, but the scene in the Shore is nothing like it is in Balboa and Laguna where the numbers run in the thousands. In Long Beach the only other time that's anything like it is T.G.I.O. week at the Long Beach State frat. houses on Ocean Boulevard. I'll probably be out looking for some action tonight myself.

"Know any parties tonight?" I ask Hutch.

"They're having their weekly bash at the Green House. It should be pretty good. They're go'n'a have a band tonight. Be a lota' flatlanders there."

The Green House is a huge two-story house that sits right on the beach down at the end of Bay Shore Avenue.

"I'm going out tonight for sure," I say. "Easter week only comes once a year in the Shore."

About then, Scrub and Floink come into the bar. They're both wearing black leather jackets, which means they're riding their motorcycles. They're wan'a be Hell's Angels, but everybody knows they're just a couple clowns putting on an act. They don't even play the role good. They don't ride Harleys; they got Ducatis. As they get close to us, Scrub shouts out,

"That really pisses me off!" And Floink laughs.

That's Scrub's favorite line. He says it whether he's pissed off or not. I've never seen him pissed off. It's kind of like his trademark saying. Sometimes he yells it so loud, he'll bring a full, noisy bar to complete silence, and when everybody sees who it is, the noise picks up again, and they all go back to what they were doing before he came in.

"What pisses you off now, Scrub?" Hutch says good-naturedly.

One And Two Halves

"We were just ridin' down Bay Shore and man, I'll tell yuh, there's lotsa' babes on the beach. What pisses me off is there's so many, it's hard to choose. Give us a pitcher and two glasses, Mike."

They get their pitcher and go back to the open pool table. We finish our pitcher off and walk out into the street. As we're going out the door, I hear Scrub yelling out from the back of the bar,

"That really pisses me off!"

As we step out onto the sidewalk, the sun hits us square in the face, and Sixto goes into a sneezing fit. When he finally stops, he says to me,

"I'm goeen down Bay Shore, check out dah rucas. See yuh in half an hour."

I unlock my bike from the meter, and Hutch and I walk to the signal and cross the street to the shop.

*　　　*　　　*

As we enter, Bernie's just finishing his last cut of the morning.

"Hey, Bernie," I say.

"Hey, Jerôme, how's it goin'?"

Hutch sits in my chair, and I put my apron on. Bernie collects the money from his client, tells him to have a happy Easter, and sweeps the floor.

"See yuh in about a half an hour," he says to me and walks out the door.

"Yuh know how we were talking about Bob Dylan over in the A.I.," I say to Hutch. "About how he's gone electric? I saw him last fall at the Hollywood Bowl."

"Really? How was it?"

51

Jerome Arthur

"Great! He did an acoustic set and an electric set. He had a great rock 'n' roll band called the Hawks backin' 'im for the electric set, but the acoustic set was just him singin', and playin' his guitar and harmonica, everything with a mic. Fans weren't too happy with the rock 'n' roll part, but they loved the stuff he did acoustic. Mood of the crowd changed when they started settin' up the band equipment and speakers. Booed 'im a little in the electric set. I thought it was a great concert. Typical Dylan. Pretty low-key. He just went out and played the songs...not a whole lota' chatter. Doesn't entertain yuh a lot between songs with jokes and small talk. Other members of the band...they just stand there and play, too. They're over in Europe right now. Wonder if the audiences over there are givin' 'im as bad a time as that audience at the Bowl gave him. What're we doin' here, Hutch?"

"Gi'me a flattop with long sides."

"Not go'n'a keep tryin' to grow it out?"

"Nah. Didn't work. Chad says I look like a pimp when my hair gets longer."

Chad's another one of our buddies. He's a guitar player and Hutch plays ukulele. They get together and play for tips at Carney's down at the Pike.

"You want it tapered in back?"

"Yeah. Low taper."

Hutch's hair's blond, wavy and medium length and thickness. It's just recently grown out from a flattop with long sides. He's been wearing the flattop since the mid-fifties when that style first got popular, and he's been the only one I've seen in years still wearing it. He tried growing it out on top, but that didn't work out, so now he wants to go back to the flattop with long sides. His mustache is reddish blond.

52

One And Two Halves

He's a native of North Long Beach, and he's been a regular fixture in the Shore since he got out of the Army. He's a charter member of Boozers Inc. That's a group that used to hang out at the A.I. in the late fifties and early sixties. They had green sweatshirts made up with that logo in gold on the back and their names, also in gold, on the front over the left breast. Hutch is probably the only member who's a local. Most of 'em are from the Midwest and other points east.

Hutch works at the phone company. He's one of the easiest going guys I know; nothing seems to bother him. One time two guys on either side of him at the bar started to duke it out, and Hutch just happened to be in the middle of it. He didn't have anything to do with the fight; he was just in the wrong place at the wrong time. A wild punch caught him off guard, and he just scrambled to get out of the way. When the dust settled, some of the other guys were telling him that he should've kicked the guy's ass, but that just wasn't his style. Like I say, too easy going for something like that.

I've got him down in the sink, and as I'm shampooing his hair, he closes his eyes. A guy who used to get his haircut from me (I think his name is John) pokes his head in the door and says,

"How yuh doing, Jerôme?"

"Fine, John." I guess that's right since he didn't tell me it wasn't. "'T's up? Been a long time. Where yuh been hidin'?"

"Been around. Still teaching. Just don't get around this way much anymore. Been getting my hair styled down at Jon Don's. How's it look?"

The nerve of the bastard, getting his hair cut somewhere else and then asking my opinion of it.

"Looks okay," I say.

Jerome Arthur

I'm just finishing up washing Hutch's hair, and he looks like he's sound asleep in the sink. Since I'm not paying any more attention to John, he turns and walks off down the sidewalk.

"You goin' out tonight?" I say as I set him back upright.

"Yeah," he says. "I'll check it out, but probably go'n'a call it an early night. I stayed out pretty late last night. Wound up across the street. Me and Gary were shootin' pool till midnight. Good thing I had today off."

"Yuh mean that truck driver thinks he's a big time hustler on the pool tables?" I say.

"Yeah. That's the one. He's actually a pretty good pool player. I like to play 'im 'cause he shoots a good stick. He's an okay guy, but sometimes he comes on a little strong. Guess that's why he doesn't have a lota' friends. He's pretty funny, smokin' his cigar and talkin' like a character outa' Damon Runyan."

That's one cool thing about Hutch. He never badmouths anybody. He just shrugs instead of saying something bad.

"You know 'im, Jerôme?"

"Nah, not really. Never actually met him; just see him around. I know who he is; he knows who I am. Thinks he's so cool, moving around the pool table calling his shots. Hey, he's a truck driver. What can I say?"

"I've known some very cool truck drivers," Hutch says.

"Yuh know, ye're right. I met one once. Back when I was in the Navy, I went on leave and did some air and ground hitch-hiking."

I worked on Hutch's hair as I talked.

"I got a hop on a transport plane from Los Alamitos, where I was stationed at the time, to Saint Louis. The flight

54

One And Two Halves

was goin' to Mc Donnell Aircraft to drop off the cap-
sule that Alan Shepherd went into space in. Soon as it was
picked up, they brought it to Los Al. and used it as a recruit-
ing tool for prospective Navy pilots. When I heard they were
transporting it to Mc Donnell, I took ten days leave and got
my name on the manifest. Once I got to Saint Louis, I was
hoping to catch another hop somewhere else. Anywhere, I
didn't care. Like I say, I was hitch-hiking. But where I really
wanted to go was Minneapolis. I got a buncha' relatives
there, and I figured if there wasn't a flight goin' that way or
anywhere else, I could always stick my thumb out on the
highway.

"So, early on that summer morning, I showed up at
operations with a gym bag full of my stuff. Any time you go
on a military flight, you're supposed to be in dress uniform,
so I was wearing my dress whites. All I had in the bag was a
couple changes of socks and scivvies, and one set of civvies
to wear out on the town wherever I might end up.

"We took off at seven-thirty in the morning. In the
air almost ten hours. Most boring flight I was ever on. Good
thing I had a *Playboy* to read. I think I read the whole damn
magazine by the time we landed. Met an Air Force sergeant
on the flight lived in Saint Louis. Said if I couldn't get a
flight outa' Mc Donnell, he'd give me a lift to a crossroads
north of town. Told me I'd get a ride from there for sure.

"Plane noise droned in my ears for half an hour after
we landed. Nice to be back on the ground. Went straight to
operations and checked on flights goin' out that night or next
morning. No traffic going out. Plane I arrived on wasn't
even leavin' till next afternoon, and it was only goin' back to
where I j'st came from."

I'm half-way through Hutch's haircut by now. He's
listening to my story. I'm running about five minutes behind
schedule. It takes time to get that flattop just right.

Jerome Arthur

"The sergeant was waitin' for me, and he gave me a lift out to Highway Sixty-one. Said if I went north on that road, it'd take me straight to Minneapolis. I thanked him and stuck my thumb out. By the time he dropped me off, it was gettin' on to dusk. Wouldn't be long and the sun'd be goin' down, and a low ground fog was coming off a river that I could hear rolling along maybe a quarter of a mile off. Kind of fog they get in Fresno in the wintertime—tule fog. Found out later that the river was the Mississippi.

"After about a half hour and not getting a ride, I was beginning to think the sergeant left me off at a bad spot. I mean, I was in the middle a' nowhere. There was a farmhouse about a quarter of a mile off the road and that was it. As the evening sky got dark, I could see in the distance the halo of lights from the small town a' Chesterfield. Fog was lying in patches over the vacant fields. Darker the sky got, the more worried I got about catchin' a ride.

"Good thing it was summer and I was in my whites, 'cause if I wasn't, I'd prob'ly still be standin' there. Nobody would 'a' seen me. I was on the side of the road, night was falling, and every time I saw headlights comin' up the highway, I stuck my thumb out. Cars were passin' me left and right, but I waited patiently, and finally a semi comes roaring up the highway. At first he passes me, and then he hits his brakes about twenty-five feet beyond where I'm standing. I picked my bag up, ran up to the cab, and opened the door. Driver was this scrawny little runt with two day's growth of beard, a cigar stickin' out of his mouth and a black slouch hat on his head.

"Asked him how far he was going, and he said Davenport, Iowa and told me to hop in. So, I threw my bag up onto the floorboard and climbed up and sat down."

56

One And Two Halves

"'Sure a good thing y're wearing that white uniform,' he said. 'Otherwise I wouldn't 'a' seen yuh. Where yuh headed?'

"Told 'im Minneapolis, and how I'd just flown in from Southern California and how I got to where he picked me up and why I was goin' to Minneapolis. He had a 'NO RIDERS' sign in the windshield, and I asked him if he'd get in some trouble for pickin' me up. He said it was his own rig and that he only put the sign up so he could choose who he wanted to pick up.

"Anyway, we rode off in the foggy night to Bowling Green and north to Hannibal, where there were all kinds of road signs and signs on houses sayin' this was Mark Twain's childhood stamping grounds. By the time we hit La Grange, north of Hannibal, it was getting late, and we were both starting to doze, so we stopped at a truck stop for our first cup a' coffee. He picked up the tab, and we got back into the truck and on the road north. I never saw so much corn in all my life, and every cornfield we passed had a little triangular sign that said, 'hybrid.'

"As the night wore on, we ran out of things to talk about, so we stared blankly at the headlight beams bouncing on the road ahead. Every once in a while the truck'd slant to the shoulder, and I'd reach over and grab the truck driver's arm. When I'd do that, he'd shake his head and come to, and then we'd start looking for someplace to get coffee. I told him I didn't know how to drive the rig, but I'd try if he wanted to get some shuteye, but he shook his head and kept driving.

"He was one hell of a truck driver for my money and one hell of a nice guy, too. Seemed interested in what I had to say, askin' me questions about myself, where I was from and how much time I had left to go in the Navy. We had a cool chat. He told me he was born and raised and still lived down in 'the Boot.' That's what they call that little section in southeastern Missouri that hangs down into Arkansas. Middle of the Ozarks.

"I know where ye're talkin' about," Hutch says.

"I couldn't believe the guy's stamina. It's true he was dozing, but mostly he was driving hard and handling the big rig like a Healey. And when sleep'd begin to overtake him, he'd pull into a truck stop or a roadside café and buy us a couple cups of coffee. He knew all the people in all the joints wherever we stopped, and they all knew him."

Bernie comes back from his lunch break just then. His first cut of the afternoon follows him in. His client's followed by Sixto, who sits down in the waiting chair opposite and picks up *Life*. Time for me to wrap this story up.

"We made it to Davenport by about eleven-thirty the next morning. He hadn't mentioned it before, and it's a good thing he didn't because I'd've been scared shitless, but he'd been awake for two days. He had two long hauls in a row and when he finished the one to Davenport, he was go'n'a take a week off. I couldn't believe it. My ass was draggin', and I'd only been awake twenty-four hours and really not doing much but sittin', and here was this scrawny, little redneck truck driver awake and workin' two days straight and still alert. He *was* looking a little haggard and tired, but he was just as feisty and full of piss and vinegar as when he first picked me up. After that night I've always had a lot of respect for truck drivers."

I'm putting the finishing touches on Hutch's haircut.

"Paul's comin' in at three today. Guess you saw 'im last night, huh?" I say.

"Yeah, he was behind the bar when I was there. Man, I've had some good times hanging with that dude. Well, *you* know. Remember the nights when we hung out in the bar after hours?"

One And Two Halves

"How could I for- get?"

"One time I went with him to a party down in Sunset Beach. He was driving and Anna was with him. Me and Crabbe were in the back seat. Him and Anna got into this big-ass fight, and by the time we got to the party, she was hangin' with me. We ended up back at my place, and when we all passed out, Anna ended up in my bed. I don't know what happened to those two guys. All I know is when I woke up in the morning, it was just her and me."

"I remember running into you two in the bar once. Was that the same time?"

"Pro'bly. That was the only time I ever went out with her."

I'm finished with his haircut, so I give him the hand mirror, and he checks out the taper and the profiles. Then he steps out of the chair and reaches for his wallet.

"Well, I'm goin' back across the street and see what's goin' on now," he says as he gives me five bucks. "See yuh later."

"Okay Hutch. I might see yuh later tonight. But if I don't, have a nice Easter."

"Thanks. You too. See yuh later, Six."

*　　　*　　　*

I'm running almost ten minutes behind schedule when Sixto Del Toro steps into my chair, and he's only my second one of the day. That means I'm go'n'a be ten minutes behind schedule for the rest of the afternoon unless I can catch up with an easier cut later on.

"Hey, Jerónimo. What's hopponeen, eh," he says.

Sixto pushes a hack downtown. He came to Long Beach, the westside, from Monterrey, México when he was a teenager during the war. Even though he was already that old

59

when he left México, he pretty much left everything there behind except his accent, and Long Beach has become the only home he's ever known. Kinda' like me and Minnesota and Los Angeles, except I was a lot younger when my parents moved out here. Even so, many's the time I've heard him say in his thick Mexican accent, "Born and raised in Long Beach, eh." He got his citizenship when he was twenty-one, shortly before he got out of the Army at the end of the war. When he came home, he moved to the Shore. Once he told me how he and his buddies used to ride the streetcar to this side of town to go to the beach when they were teenagers. He said he always liked the Shore better than the westside. They're two different neighborhoods. Mostly minorities on the westside. The Shore is all white. Sixto's the only Mexicano I know of around here.

To his neighbors he may be just "that Mexican," but he stands right alongside them as far as having the same living standards—clean neighborhoods, good schools for his kids (better than the ones he himself went to on the westside), and the leisurely, casual pace of life at the beach.

He's got two kids, a boy and a girl, and they're both smarter'n hell. The daughter's an honor student on a scholarship at one of those fancy eastern colleges, Smith or Bryn Mawr, something like that. His son, Dave, who's also a steady customer of mine, wasn't a good student like his sister, but he's a hell of a lot smarter'n either his dad or his teachers give him credit for. He didn't go to college like his sister. He joined the Army last June after he graduated from Wilson. Right now he's in Vietnam. I think the kid could've made a smarter move, like go to college, but then maybe he didn't have the grades. So, he goes off to fight in a dumb war nobody can explain, not even the people who started it (they least of all), and his dad's quite proud of him and glad he made the right decision.

One And Two Halves

"So, how's Dave doin' these days? "

"He's doeen okay, mon. Got a pretty goodt deal. Before he went to Vietnam, he was in airplane mechanics school down Fort Benneen, Georgia. Don't even carry a gun. Hal's bal's, he ain't even near any action. Just works on helicopters."

"Sounds like he lucked out."

"Yeah, I guess. Worst duty he's hadt so far was down Georgia, and there it wasn't the duty that was buggeen him; it was those southern redtnecks. They're prejudice as hal'. Around here people are prejudice too, but they ain't as open about it as down there."

"I thought they were only prejudice against chanates."

"Hal' no. Down there, they don't like nobody that ain't a paddy. Don't even like the paddies that ain't in their class. To them, Metsicans and chanates are all the same."

"Really?" I say. "Sometimes it makes you wonder what in the hell you're fightin' for, doesn't it? I mean you got'a go overseas and fight a war for your country, and you can't even walk down the street at home without getting' hassled by somebody."

"It don't make no difference to me, mon," says Sixto. "Just as long as they leave me alone, I don't care what they do to other people. It's a free country. Right?

"To a degree."

"Okay, so if some guy wants to be prejudice, that's his right, eh. I got'a right to choose the friends I wan'a hang around with, too. It works both ways. Alls Dave's got'a do is get in there and fight for his country and mind his own business, and nobody's go'n'a give 'im a badt time."

"I'm startin' to wonder what the hell we're doin' over there. I don't think it's worth it. It's phony for us to say

61

we're go'n'a give those people the American way of life when we ain't even got it ourselves."

"Wha'da yuh mean, we ain't got it? We got it better right here in this country than any other place in the world, eh. And all we're doeen is makeen sure those gooks have the same advantage. The only way we can keep on haveen it so goodt is to stick together. The individual cannot come before the country: it's like the old sayeens, 'unitedt we stand; dividedt we fall,' and, 'my country right or wrong.' People start putteen themselves above the country, it'll be anarchy, and then we'll be fighteen guerilla warfare [he used the Spanish pronunciation] right here at home, just like in Vietnam. The way I see it, Dave's got'a go over there and halp fight that war for two reasons: to keep us free over here, and to halp them over there get the same kind of freedom we got."

I don't think there's really a whole hell of a lot I can say here. I just don't agree with it. But he keeps on smiling, and I don't feel like arguing so I change the subject.

"Yuh know, I only got one more semester left after this one?"

"No kiddeen, eh," he says. "Wha'cha go'n'a do then?"

"I'm go'n'a keep on working here for a while. Got my eye on a little commercial spot down on Roycroft, just off Second. Yuh know the yarn shop in the brick building?"

Since Bernie's come back from lunch, I'm trying to keep my voice down, so he can't hear me, but I don't really have to worry because he's keeping pretty busy with Red.

"Yeah."

"Perfect size for a little two chair shop."

"How come you're not go'n'a get a job with your degree?"

One And Two Halves

"Only went to school for the education, not to get a job. 'Sides it's way too much fun doin' this. Ain't like a job. More like hangin' out with my best friends, and when they leave, they give me money. What could be more perfect?"

"You got it made, eh."

I'm finishing Sixto's haircut, and Sam, my next customer, walks in the door. He picks up the newspaper and waits his turn. I look out the front window, and I see a woman, who looks to be in her forties, walking past, her hair a beehive sprayed up, looking like cotton candy, her ass rocking back and forth in her tight mini skirt. Her legs look like toothpicks going straight down to her spiked heels. She's wearing shades and a hard scowl on her face.

"I'll tell you one thing," I say to Sixto, getting back to his haircut and our conversation. "I'm sure glad I don't have to worry about being drafted right now."

"Me too, eh!" he says. "If they recalledt me, I just plain wouldn't go. One war's enough, eh. Back in 'fifty when Korea broke out, a lota' the guys from my old outfit stayed in the reserves, and they got recalledt, but they couldn't touch me. I already hadt my discharge, and if they thought I'd go down and volunteer, they were nuts. I tol' my ol' lady to get ready to he't for the hills. I tol' her, 'I ain't goeen back for notheen.' But turns out, I hadt notheen to worry about 'cause they went 'head on and settled it after a couple years. I didn't care what anybody saidt, mon; I didt my time, and I wasn't goeen back."

"Yeah, I got my discharge two years ago. Good feeling."

It's two o'clock and I think I've gained maybe three minutes on my schedule. Sixto's haircut is really looking good. The taper is smooth and the hair is neatly trimmed over his ears with a fairly high arch, dos lineas on the neckline. On top it's barely long enough to lie down. He looks

63

like a middle age Mexicano with an Ivy League haircut. I pick up the hand mirror from the hook on the backbar. I get him lined up so he can see the reflection of the back of his head in the mirror.

"How's that look, Sixto?" I say.

"Lookeen goodt, mon," he says. "Now I can go out and dazzle the chavalas with brilliance. If I can't do that, I'll baffle 'em with bullshit, eh Jerónimo?"

I take the haircloth off, and as he stands up, his guaraches squeak on his bare feet. We walk over to the cash register together, and he gives me six bucks and asks for fifty cents change.

"I guess I'll go across the street and have another beer and then go back down the beach," he says. "Lota' young college stuff down there today, and I may as wal' enjoy it while I can, 'cause tonight I got'a go back to work."

"You look dressed for it," I say referring to his cutoffs and T-shirt."

"Okay. Happy Easter, Jerónimo," he says and turns and walks out.

"Yeah, Happy Easter, Sixto," I say to his back.

*   *   *

I turn away from the register and go over to my chair. Sam's already sitting there with the newspaper on his lap.

Sam's a swarthy guy with a thick, dark head of straight hair that he wears a little longer than my average client. He's normally got a standing appointment every other Saturday, but he's in on Friday this time because he's going out to the river tomorrow. He's an engineer, one of six guys whose hair I cut, who works for Shell Oil Company. I look at my book and can see that two more are coming in this af-

One And Two Halves

ternoon. They must all be going to the river for the Easter weekend. Sam here and Chuck McBain both have ski boats out at Parker Dam.

Sam's cut is easy because he doesn't ever want it to look like he needs a haircut or like he's just had it cut, so there's really not much to do, but that pencil-thick hair sure is hard to work on. When he first started coming to me, he was wearing a crewcut, which was a good style for him. He let it grow out when we went to shampoo cuts and raised our prices. I guess he figured he wasn't getting his money's worth when it was short.

By now I've got his hair washed, and I'm starting to cut it. He's reading the sports section of the paper.

He's built like he might've been a football player in high school and maybe even college. His arms are so muscular that they bow out over his delta-shaped flanks that taper down to a waist that's not as slim as it once was. His quiet voice and moody behavior match his stoic appearance. He never says much, but when he does, it's usually in a quiet southern accent. Joe Cockburn, one of his buddies from Shell, tells me Sam has an identical twin brother. The first time he went to Sam's apartment, he saw a picture of the brother on a bookshelf, and because he thought it was Sam, his first reaction was to think Sam was vain, but then Sam told him the picture was of his brother.

Of all of these Shell guys I cut, Sam's the one who's most to himself, quiet and private. The only time he ever had roommates was for a short time after he came to the Shore and moved into the Yellow House with Gary, Chuck and Roland. He's single but soon-to-be married. That he has a partner on his boat strikes me as quite out of character, especially since his partner, Gene, a printer, who goes straight to the want-ads whenever he picks up a newspaper, is so different from Sam.

65

Jerome Arthur

They're a real Mutt-and-Jeff combination. Whereas Sam is short, stocky and ramrod straight, Gene is tall and lanky and walks with a slouch. Sam's a sharp dresser, wearing expensive suits at work and snappy-looking sport clothes on the weekends. It's not unusual to see one of the legs of Gene's worn Levis drooping over the top of his scuffed Wellington-style boot. And he's constantly grabbing the jeans by the belt loops and hitching them up on his non-existent hips. His shirt's only half tucked in most of the time, and his thinning blond hair is always messed up. He quit coming to me when I started washing all heads before cutting them. I guess Sam keeps him as a partner because he's a good mechanic and fixes the boat when anything goes wrong with it. Sam probably doesn't know shit about working on car and boat engines and that's Gene's specialty. Sam wears a ring with the Greek letters $AT\Omega$ inscribed on it.

"I hear Chuck's moving up to San Francisco," I say. Chuck's the first one from Shell to start getting his haircut from me. All the others came to me on his recommendation. Another one of the five, Roland Dark, had told me about Chuck's promotion and transfer earlier in the week. "He got a promotion or something?"

He takes his time answering. Unlike Chuck, who seems to think hard before he answers so he won't give the wrong answer, Sam seems to think hard because he's frustrated at not having a quick answer, wrong or right.

"They say it's a promotion, and I guess it is, but it's probably a dead end. I mean, I don't think he'll go much higher, although it's possible. Doesn't work hard enough. He's in pretty good with his boss, but he just doesn't put in enough hours. With a big company like Shell, you've got to work your tail off for a few years until you get ahead a little, then you can start kissing up to your boss. Actually, one way to impress your boss is to put in a few extra hours a week.

66

One And Two Halves

The competition in the oil business is just too much to do otherwise. That's why I put in ten to twelve hours ever' day and work weekends, too. Tomorrow's the first Saturday I've had off in two months.

"I was told when I went to work on my job that nobody ever had it completely caught up. I'll probably have it all in order within a couple of months. Then you can watch me get promoted. They'll find another mess somewhere else in the company and they'll send me in to clean it up. That's the way it'll go all the way to the top, and then I'll be cleaning up the big mess—the company."

"Hope it pays off for you."

"I think it will," he says, "I just don't think schmoozing is the be all and end all for getting promoted."

That's the most I ever heard Sam say in one sitting. He usually complains once or twice about his sinus headache and then he sits still while I wrestle with his mop. What little I know about Sam, I've found out from the rest of the gang, and even they don't know much.

"You been out to Parker lately?" I say.

"We're going tomorrow, as a matter of fact. Go'n'a come home Sunday evening."

"Who all's going?"

"Gene and I are going for sure. Don't know about the others. I think Chuck and Roland and their wives are going. Kelly might be coming too."

"How about Boring and Cockburn? They ever go out with you guys?"

"I didn't invite 'em for tomorrow. Don't know if Chuck or Roland invited 'em, but they've been out before. Joe used to go all the time before he got married, but he hasn't been out lately."

"How come you always go out to the river? Like, why don't you just go down here to Marine Stadium?"

Jerome Arthur

"Oh no. I'll never put my boat in saltwater. Too hard on the metal parts of the engine. Fresh water's bad enough. 'Sides, it's too cold and too crowded down here. The water at the river's warmer, and although it's getting crowded out there too, it's not nearly as bad as here."

I'm dusting the loose hairs off the back of his neck when Gary Kelly comes in. He and Sam say hello to each other, and while they're talking, the phone rings. I answer it because Bernie's got a head in the sink and hands full of shampoo. It's Corvette.

"You got any openings today, Jerôme?"

"Nah, we're both booked up today, Mike. Wha'da yuh got?"

"Got a guy here needs a haircut today. Got any suggestions?

"I still got a couple openings tomorrow."

I can hear Mike asking the guy if tomorrow's okay. He says no and Mike comes back on the line.

"He's only in town today. Can't make it tomorrow."

"Tell 'im to check out Sam's down next door to the Belmont Theater. Those guys might have some openings. We're all booked up today."

"Okay, thanks."

"Is that about right for you, Sam?" I say, holding the hand mirror up so he can see the back and sides.

"Looks good, Jerôme," he says. "Now I'll be nice and cool tomorrow out at the river."

"I didn't take *that* much off," I say looking over at Kelly.

"You've got a point there," Sam says. "How 'bout another appointment? Say two weeks from now?"

"Sure," I say, turning to the appointment book. "How's Saturday morning sound, two weeks from tomorrow, ten o'clock?"

One And Two Halves

"'Sounds good. That should get me down to the plant early enough."

"Cool."

I give him a card with that information written on it, and he goes over to the cash register and puts down five and a half bucks.

"You coming out tomorrow?" he asks Gary.

"Nah. Susan and I are goin' up to Santa Barbara."

Sam heads out the door.

*　　　*　　　*

Gary here and Joe Cockburn, who's coming in later today, are my two coolest guys from Shell. From what I've heard from the others, Gary's the guy who really deserves a break with that company. He's tried all the ways of getting ahead that the others have tried, but none of them worked for him. He really deserves to be the fair-haired boy that Chuck McBain is and Roland Dark is trying to be, but never will be because he doesn't have the personality. Gary tried busting his ass like Sam, but he gave up because he found out early on there's no future or money in it. So now he's going to law school on the company's nickel, and when he finishes and passes the bar, he's go'n'a tell the company to get fucked. Says he wants to make something out of his future now that he's wasted four years trying without much success to climb the corporate ladder.

"How's it goin'," Jerôme?" Gary says as he sits in the chair.

"Pretty good," I say. "Burned out from goin' to school. So glad to have this week off. I needed it."

"I know what yuh mean," he says. "I'm spending a lota' time these days prepping for the baby bar. Wears yuh out."

Jerome Arthur

"How's that goin'?"

"Goin' good. Really learnin' a lot. I think I'm go'n'a like being a lawyer."

"How long you been at it now?"

"Just finishing up my second year. Like I said, I'm boning up for the baby bar. I'm taking the test this summer."

"What kind of test is it?"

"Baby bar's a test you have to take to continue in law school if the school you're goin' to isn't accredited, which is the situation where I'm going."

"So, what happens after you pass the test? How much longer yuh got'a go before you become a lawyer?"

"Two more years, and 'soon as I pass all my classes and graduate, I can take the regular bar exam. Pass that and I can practice law in California."

"Then you can tell Shell to go take a flyin' fuck, right?"

"That's the plan, and it'll be nice too, telling 'em where to go. I've done about all I'm go'n'a do for that company. I'm tired a' knocking myself out and getting nothing for it."

"How'd yuh ever get tied up with 'em in the first place?"

"I had great credentials when I graduated from college. They had recruiters on campus in my last year at Penn State, and because I had such good grades, they were really interested in me, but I didn't bite right away. Went to grad. school instead. They kept after me. Finished grad. school and went to work for 'em. Moved out here with the company.

"Everything went great until I got here and actually started working. My boss set up a competition between me and a couple of other managers. It didn't seem to matter what kinda' job I was doing; all I had to do was butter up the bosses and try to cut ev- erybody else's throat. The next thing I knew, all my best friends were doing the same thing. It was pretty stressful. I was rooming with Chuck and Roland in the same house at night and supposedly cutting their throats during the day, and they were supposed to be doing the same thing to me and to each other.

"Damn rat race! I was doing a good job, as were Chuck and Roland. So, guess what happened next? We get these quarterly evaluations. They can be really good character references and job recommendations, but it doesn't always work out that way. I wasn't doing anything any differently than anybody else. At least, I don't think I was. I mean, a person knows when he's messing things up. I was doing my job the best I could. After a while, I got my regular evaluation with all the right boxes checked, but in the section where it calls for a rating, the guy who evaluated me put down, 'Good, but needs experience.' I'd been with the company almost two years. After that much time, how much experience does a guy need?"

"Yeah, right."

"From then on things really started going downhill. I saw guys like Chuck and Roland who joined the company at the same time I did, and after, getting raises and advancements. I wasn't going anywhere. I'd had a couple articles published in professional journals; I'd been working right along and doing a good job; the people who worked with and for me said they liked me and liked working with me. I know for a fact that a couple of them even put in a good word for me with the higher-ups, but it didn't matter. I found myself in a dead-end job, and I'd always tried to do my best. So, I decided to take another road, and that's why I'm in law school."

"That's great," I say. "I hope you make it through."

"My leaving won't make any difference there. They'll never miss me. Engineers are a dime a dozen. They'll probably just get some guy outa' college they think will fit into their rut, and they'll indoctrinate him like they tried to do with me. When he wises up, if he does, he'll move on just like me."

"Wha'da the other guys think about all this?"

"Well, they're all doing well with the system, or at least they think they are. Chuck's moving up, and Sam's so damn busy putting in hours, that he doesn't even realize he's being used. He's on salary for God sakes. All the hours he puts in, he probably only makes four bucks an hour."

"Really! God, I make more'n that cuttin' hair."

"Really. And if Joe gets a couple more articles published, which is very likely, he'll be able to name his price with anybody. You know he's one of only a couple of experts in logging on the west coast. He's really into his job. I wouldn't be surprised if he became president, if not of Shell, then at least of some other oil company. He's bright but he's also a sleeper. Everybody's making a big deal out of Chuck's promotion. Cockburn's the one to watch. He's got more going for him on paper than Chuck. Chuck's only advantage seems to be that people like him a lot. Oh, he knows what he's doing all right, but so did Willy Loman and what did it get him?"

"You ain't kiddin' there."

"You've got to eventually have more going for you than to be well-liked."

"I guess that's true. Sure a lot more to it than what meets the eye. How's that look, Gary?" I say, holding up the hand mirror so he can see the back and sides.

"Looks good," he says.

Then I hang the hand mirror back on its hook and dust his neck off.

One And Two Halves

"That's a good- looking haircut," I say. "I think I'll fiber glass it and put it on display in the window."

He laughs, gets out of the chair and walks over to the cash register. As he's paying me, he invites me to a party at his house tonight.

"It'll be fun. All the other guys'll be there with their wives and girlfriends, plus some other friends you may or may not know. Maybe you can get some new customers."

"I might check it out. See how it goes."

"Well, come if you can."

"Okay, Gary. See yuh later."

*   *   *

As he walks out, my next cut, Paul Shultz, passes him on his way in.

Paul sits down, and I slip the haircloth over his shoulders and set him up for the shampoo. He wears his thin hair in an Ivy League style, short on the sides and just long enough to lie down on top. No part. I ask him how he wants it. You never know when somebody's go'n'a change his mind at the last minute and quit sporting the hairstyle he's been wearing since I've been cutting it.

"How come you always ask me that? You know how I like it. Just cut it."

"Okay."

Paul's the night bartender at the A.I. Like Hutch said, we've had some pretty good times with him. Once we stayed in the bar after hours shooting pool and drinking beer till dawn. We left at daybreak and went down to the end of Belmont Pier. It was a beautiful morning, the sunrise a symphony orchestra, the eastern horizon a kaleidoscope of colors veiled in the morning mist, all purple and pink, red and orange, as the sun broke over it.

Jerome Arthur

"Hutch was in at one o'clock. He was telling me about the time you guys went to a party in Sunset Beach, and how he ended up with your date."

"Oh yeah, I remember that night," he says. "Anna bad-mouthed me and came after me. Punched me in the mouth. Split my lip. All I did was try to fend her off. He tell yuh that?"

"Didn't give me the details. Just said you two got in a fight."

I finish washing his hair and move the chair back upright. I'm in the groove now. Four down. Four to go.

"What's new?" I say.

His thin, wet hair is plastered against his head, showing his white scalp.

"Not much. Just fillin' pitchers and mugs for the clientele. Lookin' for another job. No future in bartending. Too much of a head scene."

"I believe it," I say. "Maybe yuh ought'a think about takin' some classes at City.

"Ain't into goin' back to school. Don't wan'a be hangin' with a buncha' bubblegummers. City ain't nothin' but a high school with ashtrays."

"Hey, it's a good school and it's free. I'm gettin' ready to graduate from State, and City's still been the best part of my college education. I don't see how you c'n go wrong. Even two years'll get yuh a better job than the one you got. That, or you can get a trade like me. I'm so glad I got this. 'Soon's I get my degree next January, I'm go'n'a start looking seriously for someplace to open my own shop."

Anytime I start talking about opening my own place, I try to keep my voice down so Bernie can't hear.

"Yeah, you got your thing worked out real good. And you're right about City," he says, "but I just ain't got the ambition to go to school. I could no more compete with

74

those young kids in the class- room than I could on the gridiron. They'd run circles around me. Hell, I have enough trouble eighty-sixin' guys my own age outa' the bar. 'Fact, I almost threw Scrub out last night. Were you there?"

"Nah. Stayed home last night. Went to bed about midnight."

"Yuh didn't miss much," he says. "Scrub was doin' his usual thing."

"I saw Scrub with Floink over there today at lunchtime."

"He got pretty wasted last night."

"And yuh eighty-sixed 'im?"

"Nah. He left on his own. No help from me. Him and Chappy got together and started buyin' pitchers."

"And there was no stoppin' 'em after that, right?"

"So to speak," Paul says. "After the second pitcher, both of 'em were on their asses. Then the place started gettin' crowded, and they were screamin' along with the music and yellin' at the girls."

"I'm surprised you didn't eighty-six the bastards. Was me, you probably would've, and permanently, too."

"That's bullshit and you know it," Paul says. "Cox might've, but you know damn well I wouldn't've. So, let me finish tellin' yuh. Scrub got carried away. The usual running-for-mayor-of-Belmont-Shore bullshit. He was standin' down at the end of the bar by the fireplace next to where Larry was sittin', but by then Larry was gone. Don't know if Scrub ran him out or if he was just tired and left. Scrub was yellin' about how he wanted everybody there to vote for him. I finally told him to keep it down. So then he yells, '*That* really pisses me off!' like he always does."

"I'm surprised you let 'im slide."

"He sat down like I told him, but not for long. Next I saw 'im, he was over hanging with Rus and Joanie, buggin'

Rus, tryin' to get him to play Cardinal Puff. Rus don't give a damn about Cardinal Puff. He was just tryin' to get Scrub to buzz off. I guess he thought if he ignored him, maybe he'd split, but that just made Scrub all the more pushy. He started hustlin' Joanie with Rus sittin' right there. Meanwhile, Cox came in going, 'Hey, uh, bad guy,' and makin' that farting sound he always makes. When Scrub pushed Rus far enough, Rus got up and pushed back, and he was so drunk that he fell on his ass. Cox, not knowin' what was goin' on before he got there, eighty-sixed Rus from the bar."

"He sure made the wrong move there, huh?"

"No shit, but that wasn't the half of it. As Rus was leaving, he tried to drag Joanie with 'im, but guess what! She wouldn't leave. Instead, she stuck around and hung with Scrub, and as far as I know, she went home with 'im, drunk on his ass and all."

It's getting close to three-thirty, and my next customer, Randall Fritz, has just now walked in. I'm halfway through the afternoon. All I've got'a do to Paul is dust off his neck and let him go.

"You don't work tonight, huh Paul?" I say taking the haircloth off.

"Nope," he says, getting up from the chair. "I ain't working tonight so I'm goin' home and listenin' to some Miles Davis, and goin' to bed early 'cause I got'a get up early to go sailing with Darryl."

"Goin' up to your folks's house on Sunday?"

"Nah, that's a drag," he says. "If there's a good wind tomorrow, we might go out again on Sunday."

"Is Darryl still living on that guy's boat?" I say.

"Yeah. George's thirty-five-foot yawl. Darryl's George's skipper. He's got the coolest gig. All he does is little odd jobs here and there, and for that he gets to live aboard and take the boat out anytime he wants to, except when George comes down to go sailing himself."

"You say, 'George comes down.' Doesn't he live around here?"

"Uh, uh. Lives in Arcadia, and only gets down here every couple months."

I guess the guy hasn't figured Darryl out yet. He's one of the biggest phonies I ever met. One night when I was sitting at the bar, I watched him toothpick some herring or something out of a pickling jar and say,

"This is what my countrymen eat."

His self-righteousness was sickening, sitting there behind his Scandinavian blond hair and scrubby beard. I guess no matter how much bread you got, it don't necessarily make you smart enough to see through guys like Darryl. I'm surprised Paul even gives him any credibility. We walk over to the cash register together, and he gives me five bucks even and says,

"See yuh around, Jerôme. Have a nice Easter."

"Okay, Paul. You too."

And he's gone.

*   *   *

I'm getting a little tired. Only four cuts left to do, and I'm starting to watch the clock. Of course, there'll be the inevitable guy who walks up to the door at five o'clock wantin' to get a haircut just when we're about to close the blinds and lock up. I shouldn't've stayed up so late last night.

It really doesn't matter how tired I am. I just love doing this. Not the work part of it so much as the hanging-out-with-my-friends part of it. I can't think of anything better. I mean, this has been a very cool afternoon so far, and

77

the fun's not over yet. Jorge, my last appointment, will no doubt bring in a six-pack, and that'll be a nice touch at the end of the day.

Randall Fritz is in the chair, and I'm sweeping up the hair I've cut since I got here. Bernie's finishing up on his two-thirty, and his three o'clock, an old drunk they call Stew, is waiting in the chair up in the front window.

I'd say Randall's about two years older than I. He was a poli. sci. major at State, and after he got his degree a couple years ago, he went to work as a parks and rec. director for the city of Westminster. He says his ultimate goal is to be a city manager. It's okay with me, as long as he sticks in the area and keeps on coming to me for haircuts. His line of work, he'll always have the bread, and he'll have to keep up on his grooming, too. He's one of my favorite clients. Money's no object, and he never complains about my work. In fact, he's sent me a few new customers who've been just as cool as he is.

"How's your job doin'?"

"Not bad. Sure is nice to be out of school. Seems like it took me forever to get through, and I ended up with a good job."

"That's great. Let me tell yuh, nothing beats liking what you do to earn your bucks."

"Really."

I'm cleaning up the design line and trimming his sideburns. He's just starting to put some style into his hair, after what has been a long time of butch-waxed crewcuts. He's go'n'a be one of the first middle class guys to wear the longer hair that you only see young student radicals and rock 'n' roll bands wearing now. He's already wearing it down over the tops of his ears. Each time I cut it, I leave it a little longer. As I finish cutting with the shears and get ready to

One And Two Halves

pick up the clippers, a tall, slim, good-looking gal walks in and stands opposite my chair.

"Hi, honey," Randall says.

I say, "Hello."

"Hi," she says and beams out a beautiful smile.

"I didn't get it down at that end of Second Street," she says to Randall, pointing west. "I'm go'n'a go look at the other end. How long will you be?"

"Don't know. How long, Jerôme?"

"About another ten minutes."

"Will you have enough time," Randall says to her.

"I think so," she says and heads for the door saying over her shoulder, "I'll be back in a few minutes."

"Okay," Randall says.

She leaves, and, man, does she look good! Bernie stops what he's doing and watches her walk out. His client looks like he's embarrassed. I hope she comes back before I finish Randall's cut.

"Where'd you meet yer wife?" I say after she's gone.

"Up at State. We had a class together. I asked her out, and one thing led to another. She's really a neat lady. I'm lucky I found her."

"Seems nice," I say. "Pretty, too."

"Like I say, I got lucky."

"How long you guys been married?"

"Since last summer. We waited till I got my job and was working for a while. Pat's still in school. She'll get her elementary teaching credential in June. She's interviewed for teaching jobs in Long Beach and Garden Grove. It'd be great if she could get a job in either district."

"It'll be cool. You'll have it made. Then you won't *even* wan'a talk to me," I kid him.

Jerome Arthur

"You're my barber. I'll always be coming here or wherever you are. You give me the best haircuts I've ever had."

And that makes my day, not to mention the money part of it. It's really amazing how some of your customers can be really nice guys and others can be real jerks. I guess it's like the rest of the world.

"'Time you get off, Jerôme?"

"I got a couple more cuts after you. The last one's go'n'a bring a six-pack with him, so I'll have a beer with him and Bernie and his last cut. Prob'ly get out'a here about a quarter to six or so. Why, what's up?"

"When you finish my haircut, Pat and I are go'n'a go downtown, do some shopping at Buffums and Desmonds. Then I thought we'd come back to the Shore. Maybe go across the street and have a beer. That should be around the time you get off. Wan'a join us?"

"Sounds cool. I should be able to get over there by six, six-thirty the latest."

"That's about the time we'll be there. We're only go'n'a have one beer, so we're not hanging around too long."

"I'll try to get outa' here quick as I can after my last cut."

I've gotten his hair dried, and I'm showing him the back in the hand mirror.

"How's that back look?" I say.

"Looks good. Thanks a lot."

Just then Pat comes back in the shop, and the two of them head out the door.

*   *   *

80

One And Two Halves

They   pass   Peter Gunn on their way out. His name is Peter González, but he likes to be called Peter Gunn. It's probably been five years since that series was on T.V. He's got one eye that's only half open. It's either glass or it's a slow eye. I've never asked, and he's never volunteered anything about it. He's a cool guy. Funny as hell. I first met him at the A.I. He's not a Boozers Inc. "member" like Hutch, but he hangs around with that crowd. He doesn't go that far back. He's even more recent than I am. He came to the Shore from Sierra Madre with Lowen when he bought the A.I. from Lon, who was the owner when I started hanging out there. Peter worked relief for Mike and Paul. Lowen never tended bar the whole time he owned the place. He preferred to play the big shot bar owner. Which is strange because the A.I. is just a run-down college beer bar. Not classy enough to act big shot about.

Lowen's long gone now. He sold the bar to Cox and moved to México, or so he said when he left, to get into the furniture import/export business. Peter stuck around and married Inez, Corny's and Yuki's ex-roommate. That's his connection to the Boozers Inc. crowd. Corny and Yuki are charter members. I can't help thinking Lowen left him holding the bag here. I'm sure Lowen doesn't owe him any money or anything like that, but somehow I get the feeling Lowen talked him into moving down here and then split on him. Peter's never said anything about it.

He grew up in a rough part of Los Angeles, Chinatown, not far from my old stamping grounds. I know how rough that neighborhood is because the high school I went to was only two blocks north of there on Bishops Road off North Broadway. I worked in cafeterias right in the center of downtown, which is only a couple miles from Chinatown.

Peter carries the reminders of his barrio upbringing. He has a crude cross with god signs tattooed on the back of his right hand just above the webbing between his thumb and forefinger, and an equally crude "A" tattooed on his left hand in the same place. When I was a kid growing up, we used to call guys with those kind of tattoos pachucos. You'd see 'em wearing French toe shoes, khaki trousers and long-sleeve Pendleton-style shirts with all the buttons buttoned and not tucked in. They had long hair squared at the nape with a ducktail and long sideburns. I can just picture Peter in his pachuco days. He talks pretty fast and is such a joker that sometimes you can't tell whether he's kidding you or not. He's a natural born salesman.

I put the haircloth over him and start shampooing his hair. He never puts anything on it, so it's usually pretty clean when I cut it, but the sebaceous glands in his scalp work overtime, so he has a hell of a time trying to keep from looking greasy. Once he told me that no matter what he wore or how often he took a shower, he still looked dirty. His style is the two-line haircut, or dos lineas as the vatos from his old barrio would call it, which is just a regular haircut with medium sideburns, but the outline over the ears comes down straight and sharp in the back on both sides with two distinct lines framing a tapered neckline. I rinse the shampoo out and move the chair back up into the upright position. As soon as I get him sitting up, he starts talking. He's like my dad; he can talk to anybody.

"You're looking rather poorly," he says, reading the classroom fatigue in my eyes.

"Doesn't surprise me that you noticed. Had a rough night last night, but not what yuh think. I's up late studying for my English midterm which is coming up on Monday."

"Boy, you're really getting serious about school, huh?"

One And Two Halves

"Not that serious. I do wan'a get good grades, but it ain't like I got a goal for when I graduate. I'm just go'n'a keep on cuttin' hair."

"Really? Don't yuh wan'a get a schoolteacher's job or something else where you can use your education?"

"Nah. Not really. I kinda' like what I'm doin' right now. 'Sides, I can already see the kind of political bullshit that goes with bein' a teacher. Can't really do what you want, like I can do here."

Just about then, Bernie pipes in from his chair, saying to Peter,

"I been tryin' to tell 'im he should do something with his education, but he ain't listenin' to me."

"Really, what's the point of getting an education if you're not go'n'a use it to get ahead," he says, half to Bernie, half to me.

"I'm goin' to college 'cause I wan'a learn. I got a special clientele, and I think it's 'cause a' my education."

"My mamá wouldn't never let me forget it if I didn't use whatever education I got."

"So, I guess she wasn't too happy when you were tending bar."

"That's right, but she understood that it was a business arrangement. I was eventually supposed to be partners with Lowen, but it didn't work out. Where I come from, education's your ticket out. The Metsicans that live in Downey and Bellflower and Pico Rivera and Whittier all came from East L.A., and most of 'em are college educatedt. They're the ones call themselves Spaniards."

I can hear the sarcasm in his tone.

"And that's how you got out?" I say.

"Yup, but I only picked up two years of college," he says. "Went to East L.A.J.C. I was lucky, though. I was hanging with a street gang when I was fifteen/sixteen. A

83

couple times I almost got my ass killed. I was with Alpine in 'fifty-four, night they marched on Macy. See this 'A'?"

He shows me the crude, homemade tattoo on his left hand.

"Everybody in the Alpine gang hadt one tattooed on their hand. Night we marched on Macy, we hadt the whole gang together, plus some veteranos. Hadt some vatos as old as twenty. I'll never forget that night. Some of the guys brought chains with locks on the end. A couple guys hadt zip guns.

"Our leader's name was Chapángui, and he calledt the organizing meeting for nine o'clock. Everybody hadt to say where they were go'n'a run. It was about that time that I started wiseen up. I said I'd run at the back of the pack. I didn't wan'a get killed, and I didn't wan'a kill nobody. The only reason I was even there was 'cause I was in love with this girl, Josie, and I wanted to show her how badt I was. Yuh know, when you're that age, yuh do some stupidt stuff.

"A year later some veterano from Macy knocked her up—she was only sixteen—so it endedt up I was shoween off for notheen. Last time I saw her, she hadt ten kids and she was still under thirty. I felt sorry for her.

"We were all getting organized for the big rumble, and the guys with knives were all goeen to run at the front. The guys with chains and locks were runneen in the middle, and us guys with just fists ran at the back a' the pack.

"After everybody got organized, we went over to the vacant lots on Mission Road to duke it out. They hadt about twelve guys, and we hadt fifteen. Everybody was weareen leather jackets and two pair of trousers and, any of us that hadt them, big heavy boots. We started marcheen and some zip guns went off up in front. But the guys shooteen them were only fireen up in the air. Most of the guys there were just as scared as me. I don't think they really meant to hurt

84

anybody. It was just a few, guys that act like criminals no matter what, eggeen the rest of us on.

"The whole scene was enough to make you sick. Most of us were scared to death, and we were the ones who were getteen hurt; the punks in the crowd filled the night with sounds of violence and hate. The front lines really started to get into it. Chains were circleen in the air and stoppeen abruptly on someone's shoulder or head. You could hear shrieks and screams. And there was a tangle of arms and legs as fists were flying. Guys with knives were pairing off and dancing around, each afraid to make the first thrust.

"The inevitable happened. Someone managed to get a zip gun reloaded and fired into the crowd. Ruben Alarcón went down. That scared the hell outa' most of us, so I took off. I don't know if anybody stuck around to help him or what happened after that. I tried to make it home as fast as I could. The whole time I was tryin' to get home, I could hear sirens in the night.

"I didn't even make contact with anybody. Like I say, I was lucky, but a lot of the other guys weren't so lucky. Ruben, the guy got shot, died. Lota' other guys got cut up pretty badt. My best buddy got hit on the head by a lock on the end of a chain. It was a badt scene—my first and last gang fight."

I noticed how his language changed. When he first started talking he was using standard American English, but about halfway through and to the end he was talking Chicano English.

"Wow! 'Sounds bad."

"It was, and after that the heat was on, so I kept a low profile for a while. A lota' vatos were questioned by the cops, but nobody must've mentioned my name, 'cause no cops ever asked me any questions.

Jerome Arthur

"I'll tell yuh one thing though, I never hung around with those vatos after that. I went 'head on and graduated high school and went two years to East L.A.J.C. Then I started job shopping aircraft parts, and that's what I been doeen ever since, except that little stretch with Lowen across the street."

"Aren't you glad you got out?"

"No doubt. Now I got a good wife (a gavacha to boot) and family and two cars, and pretty soon we're go'n'a buy a new house out in Orange County—all the things I ever wanted. Then all I'll need will be a color T.V. and stereo with a tape deck. I could watch football on Sunday and listen to music the rest of the time. What else do I need, eh?"

Our conversation is interrupted by the loud voice of the guy in Bernie's chair.

"Hey, didn't I tell you not to skin the sides?"

Peter and I both look over at Bernie and his customer, but then we look away. What a jerk that guy is. He's a junior high school teacher I tried to get in my chair once when I first came to work here, before we started doing shampoo cuts and going by appointment.

"You're probably a pretty good barber," he'd said, "but it's like asking me if I would rather have steak or ribs. You put the two of them together, and if I want steak, I want steak. There's no particular reason behind it."

What a lame explanation, and besides, who cares? I'm booked now. I've got more than I can handle, and I don't need his business. As many cuts as I'm doing today, I'm not looking for any extras. And I really do hate it when people drop out. I see them for half an hour once every couple, three weeks for two or three or four years, and just when I get to know them, they disappear, like Chuck McBain. I've only been cutting his hair for maybe three years tops.

One And Two Halves

Bernie's one of the few people I know who's really settled. Been running this shop for over twenty years and married to the same woman for just as long, but he ain't very happy. He's got somethin' happenin' on the side. He doesn't think I know about Trisha, but I do. I'm surprised his wife Madge hasn't figured it out yet. And then again maybe she has.

I'm putting the finishing touches on Peter's haircut, so I ain't saying much now. Just then, Chad, Bernie's next customer comes in, and he comes over to my chair.

"Hey Jerôme, Peter," he says and shakes Peter's hand.

"Hey, Chad, 's happenin'?" we both say almost in unison."

"How're you guys doin'?"

"Not bad."

"Good."

"Looks like Bernie's ready for me. See yuh later."

He gets into Bernie's chair.

When I finish cutting Peter's hair, he invites me to go with him next door for a cup of coffee, but I tell him I can't because Joe Cockburn has just walked in. Then Peter says the next time he sees me at the A.I., he'll buy me a beer.

*   *   *

That's it. I collect my five bucks and turn him loose. Joe Cockburn gets in the chair. The third and last one today from Shell. Then Jorge and I'm done.

"How's it goin', Joe?"

"Great. How 'bout you?"

"Can't complain. Wouldn't do me any good if I did. Saw Gary and Sam earlier."

"Oh yeah? How're those guys doin'?"

87

"Not bad. Gary invited me to his party tonight. You goin'?" I say as I recline him into the sink.

"Yeah, I'll be there. We're getting a babysitter. I'm taking the wife out to dinner, and then we're coming up here to the party. How about yourself? You go'n'a go?"

"Prob'ly. I'm thinkin' about it."

"You should," he says. "Gary's parties are always good. He's got a lot of friends, and he always invites some fine-looking ladies, too. That doesn't do *me* much good, but it's great for you single guys."

"Sounds good. I might go. Lota' Easter Week parties around the Shore tonight and tomorrow."

"Oh, to be single," he says with a sigh. "When you get married, you don't just line your parties up. Only party in town is the one in front of the boob tube. Soon as the wife gets the kid in bed, she gets her flannel nightgown and terry cloth robe on and sits in front of the tube reading a book. Next thing yuh know she's sound asleep on the couch. Then she gets up, and without even saying good night, she drifts off and goes to bed. That's married life. Just remember it when you think you might wan'a tie the knot."

He's chuckling as he's talking.

"Yeah, think I know what yuh mean."

"Don't get me wrong. Most of it's good, but it's like any routine. Gets boring, just like anything you're go'n'a be doing for the rest of your life. Work's like that, too, but occasionally you get transferred, so that gives you some variety. In marriage you don't get transferred." He laughs. "It's the same lady for the rest of your life."

Cockburn's a good guy. My only client who asks me to thin out the top. I don't normally like to use the thinning shears, but with Joe it's a must. The top's so damn thick and bumpy from the wave pattern that I've got'a do it. One time I tried to skip it, and it just didn't work out.

One And Two Halves

As I'm lathering up his hair, he lets out a long sigh and then he says, "Best part of my day. Wouldn't mind getting a shampoo every day. Sure is relaxing."

"It's only two bucks for just a shampoo," I say. "You ought'a do it. I could fit you in."

"Are you kidding? I couldn't afford that much every day."

I can't argue with that, but I'd be willing to bet he spends that much or more on his lunch every day. I guess lunch is more important to him than getting a shampoo. And then, maybe he brown bags it. His eyes are shut; he looks completely relaxed. Right now, I could charge him anything and he'd pay. I could dig having someone shampooing my hair right now, somebody like Sophia Loren, maybe.

I glance past Bernie out the front window. The sidewalk on our side of the street is totally in shade. The sun is reflecting on the orange sign above the door of the A.I. Both sides of the street are still fairly crowded, but there aren't too many bikinis out now. It occurs to me that I haven't looked out the front window much today. I guess I didn't miss much. No matter. I'm suddenly aware of how isolated we all are from each other—Cockburn in the sink with his eyes closed, Bernie hovering over his customer, and the crowd out in the street moving along, each in his own world. Soon I'll be out there, too.

As I lift Cockburn out of the shampoo bowl, he shrugs and says, "Boy, that was refreshing. You could've left me down there. I wouldn't complain."

"Yeah, that's the hard part. Now comes the easy part."

As I start to cut, he says, "Make sure you thin it out good on top."

"Okay," I say. "By the way, I saw Roland earlier in the week, and he says Chuck's getting transferred up north. Sam and Gary both confirmed it a little while ago."

"That's right, and it's a good thing, too."

"Oh yeah? How come? You glad to see him go? Thought you guys were buds."

"We are. Exactly why I'm glad. It's a big break for him, and he deserves it, but I'm also glad to see him go because if he sticks around here, there's go'n'a be trouble between him and Bill Boring. You know Boring, Particular Bill?"

"Yeah," I say. "Do I ever! He's one of my hardest customers to please. "What's up between Chuck and Particular Bill? I didn't even think they knew each other that well."

"They don't, but they're getting acquainted. You *do* know that Particular Bill's got wedding plans with one of the secretaries down at work, don't you?"

"I knew he was planning on getting married, but I didn't know she worked for the company. So what? He marries a gal from the plant. What's the big deal?"

"Normally it wouldn't mean anything, but this gal's been playing around with Chuck."

"Really? I thought Chuck was married."

"He is. What difference does that make? You ought'a see Boring's fiancé. A real knock-out. And tonight, if you go to Gary's party, you'll get to see it live. Chuck and his wife'll be there; so will Particular Bill and his fiancé."

"Yeah? I might make it after all, but do I really *want* to? You tell me."

I'm just jiving. I'm probably go'n'a go for sure, now.

"Yuh ought'a. Parties in that house are always great, ever since Gary and Chuck and Roland first started living there. Before we all got married, I used to live down the street, so I've been to just about every party they've ever had there."

With a patronizing smile on his face, Asa pokes his head in the front door and says to Bernie, "It's a quarter after four, Bernard. They'll be starting up pretty soon."

"I'm glad you reminded me," Bernie says. "I almost forgot all about it. Excuse me, Chad, I'm go'n'a set up the T.V. so we can watch the feature race."

He walks past my chair to the back room, pushes the T.V. out, and plugs it in at the rear of the shop.

As he's turning it on, he says to no one in particular, "Feature race is on. Can't miss that."

Then as he heads back toward his chair, he looks my way and flashes that goddamn smile where you can see the gold crowns in the back of his mouth.

"You a racing fan, Joe?" I say.

"Nah, that's something that never appealed to me. Actually, I'm not much of a sports fan at all."

"Bernie turns on the feature race every Friday. He used to have a pool, but people lost interest and weren't buying chances on it, so he gave it up. He's crazy about the ponies. You know he used to be a jockey? Those pictures are of him."

I point at the two enlarged, framed snapshots near the door to the back room. One shows the photo finish of Bernie riding a thoroughbred; the other has him sitting on the same garlanded horse in the winner's circle.

"Oh really? Didn't know that. I've seen the pictures before, but never knew who it was."

"Yeah, it's Bernie. He was only about eighteen or nineteen when they were taken."

"How come he got out of it? Money wasn't good enough for 'im?"

91

Jerome Arthur

"Nah, it wasn't that. 'Fact, he says he made more money then, in the middle of the damn Depression, than he ever made in his life. Says when people are broke like they were then, they'll buy a pari-mutuel ticket before they'll buy food for their family. Reason he quit was 'cause he put on weight. Says when he was in training, all he'd eat all day long was a lettuce and tomato salad with some vinegar over it. No wonder jockeys're so damn little."

"You ought'a come to the party, Jerôme," he says, changing the subject back to what we were talking about before. I'm working over the top of his head with the thinning shears. "You'll have a good time; I guarantee it."

As I finish Cockburn's haircut, Joe Hernández announces the entries.

"Stick around and watch the race," I say.

"Okay," he says.

My last customer, Jorge Ballesteros, comes in early for his appointment right at that moment.

"Lookss like I got here jusst in time for the horsse race," he says.

Jorge has walked past my chair and is standing off to the side near the television set. He's wearing shiny, tight swim trunks, and you can see his dick forming a rounded hump behind the fabric. His short-sleeve Hawaiian print shirt is unbuttoned and hanging open. He's got a paper sack about the size of a six-pack tucked under his arm, and he offers one to everybody in the shop. Everyone but Cockburn and Mister Nims, Bernie's next customer, takes one.

As the race is about to begin, Bernie, Chad, Mister Nims and Asa are standing in a semi-circle around Bernie's chair looking at the T.V. Joe Hernández announces, "There they go," and for the next two minutes the shop's all a-bustle with the different people watching the race. Shortly after the winner, Kauai King, crosses the finish line and we've all

92

seen the photo finish a couple times, Joe Cockburn, and Asa go out the front door. Chad finishes his beer and leaves. That leaves Bernie and me alone with our last customers of the day, Jorge and Bradley Nims. Bernie turns the T.V. off and rolls it into the back room.

*   *   *

By the time Jorge sits in the chair, I'm all in. Up late, studying for the midterm on Monday. Spent the morning in the library, and the afternoon cuttin' hair. Jorge's brought in a six-pack of Budweiser bar bottles, and the ice-cold beer really hits the spot. I've been cuttin' Jorge's hair for a couple years now. He's out of the closet and pretty open about his homosexuality. It's amazing how quickly things are changing with that issue. He teaches fifth grade down in Newport, and I'm sure his colleagues are aware of his sexual preference. Five years ago, he wouldn't have been so open about it. He's little and fragile-looking and he even kind of swings his hips when he walks. He's a cool guy, and who the hell cares if he's queer or not? What the hell, he never goes after me, so I ain't sweatin' it.

"How're things in Balboa?" I say. He lives on the island.

"Fine," he says with a little movement of his eyebrow and a petite shrug of his shoulders. His esses have a strong sibilant sound. "I've had a couple of my sstudentss sstaying with me for the week, and boy, have they kept me busy. They left thiss morning to sspend Easster with their families."

Jorge bought a house on Balboa Island shortly after he started teaching in that district. Sometimes students spend weekends and school holidays with him. I wonder what those parents think about the kids's sleepovers with their

93

thirty-five-year-old teacher. I know the guy, and so what if he is a fruit? He ain't a pedophile. I trust him, but do the parents of those kids trust him? I guess they do. He's so open about it that they've got'a know he's gay.

"Boy, I'll tell yuh, Jorge, this brew you brought in sure hits the spot. It's been a long day."

"I abssolutely agree. It *does* tasste good after I've been on the crowded beach all day in the hot sun. Not that I'm complaining, mind you. Easster week last year, I was in a town in Oregon called Gold's Beach. Yuh ever been to Oregon, Jerôme?"

"Not really. I hear they don't like Californians up there. If that's true, I don't think I'd care to go."

"I've heard that. I think they're just jealouss of our warm weather and nice beaches. Gold's Beach is a cold and windy place, foggy too. Miserable. Not nearly as nice as any of our beaches. Couple of my friends and I were walking our dogs on the beach up there. We were all bundled up against the cold, but it wasn't enough. We had to get out of the weather if we were ever go'n'a get warm. It was lunchtime so we went looking for a resstaurant."

"I know what yuh mean. I hate it when it's cold at the beach."

"So here we ah...were at this little redneck cafe in the little redneck town of Gold's Beach. We'd just come from the beach and we'd brought these dogs, and there were three of us, uh, each with a little frou-frou dog and a..."

"A little frou-frou dog, eh?" I'm laughing.

"Yeah...and a Lincoln Continental. And we stopped...we'd just come from the beach. We'd walked the dogs. And there we were in this little town. We came to this cafe, and I don't remember the name of the cafe. We called it the Blue Haze Café 'cause the cigarette smoke was so heavy. Anyway, we pulled up in front, and we noticed...and there

One And Two Halves

were...it   was   all   win- dows...how everybody sort of went...lookin'... here's these three guys, a Lincoln Continental and three frou-frou dogs."

"Three frou-frou dogs!" I've shut the clippers off, I'm laughing so hard.

"And uh...they looked at us as we pulled in, and we got out of the car. We went into this cafe, and it was literally a blue haze...."

"Of smoke?"

"Of smoke. Everybody smoked...."

"In that place?"

"Everybody smoked, and uh, they were all looking at us."

"They were all a buncha' rednecks...?"

"Oh, redneckss big time, and after they all kinda' got over the shock, the waitress came over and said, 'three of yuh?' I said, 'yess.' So, she took us down to the other end of the...to thiss, to thiss...it musst've been the, uh, cook's table...yuh know what I mean, the resstaurant people's table...?"

"Yeah?"

"It was off to the side where everybody could ssee...everybody was sstaring at thiss table...sstaring at uss. But, uh, we finished, got up, and each new persson that came in...you could tell the locals, their mouths moving and then they'd look at uss. Ha ha! We were the goofiesst...."

"Yeah." I'm really cracking up, now. "'See them queers come in over there?'"

"Three queers and their little dogs!"

"Their little frou-frou dogs. That's great!"

"We finished and I told Gilbert and Charles, I said, 'Now we have to walk the dogs up and down in front of the restaurant.'"

"A parade," I laugh. "Do a parade. Yeah."

"Gilbert and Charles were both saying, 'let's get out of here. I don't feel comfortable here...these people here aren't....' I told 'em, 'let me have the dogs.' I walked up the sstreet a block and down the sstreet a block...and, uh, got in the car, and that gave them ssomething to talk about the next three or four days."

"And this is where? Gold's Beach? Is that it?"

"Yess. A morbid little town, but I...I've got it all written down."

"You wrote it all down?"

"Yess, I did a...when I travel I do a journal."

"Well, that sounds like fun. 'Sounds like you had a good time. And that was last year, you said?"

"Yess, last Easster."

"The Blue Haze Cafe," I say, shaking my head.

"Oh, God yess. And I haven't been to Oregon ssince then."

"Another bummer about Oregon is it's out in the sticks."

"You can ssay that again. I missed the crowds as well as the warm weather."

"Yuh sure can't say the Shore and Balboa ain't got their share of crowds."

"That'ss true. If you want to...a crowd, just go to a dollar drown across the sstreet ssometime."

"Yeah, but that's too much of a crowd for my money. Too much hassle. That used to be a neat thing when they first started it. Used to be you could go and only locals'd be there, but now they come from all over, from as far away as Wilmington. Not what it used to be."

"I went lasst Ssunday. Firsst time for me. Didn't know anything about it. Jusst happened to stop in for a beer, and they assked me if I wanted to join in on the drown. I

One And Two Halves

uh...didn't   know...what   it was. Bartender ssaid it's all the beer you can drink in two hours for just one dollar."

"How'd you like it? Was it a cool crowd? Anybody get outa' line?"

"It was fun. Crowded, though. When it sseemed like it couldn't hold another person, two or three more would walk in. In an hour and a half, I got ssix beers for a dollar. Couldn't've stayed much longer. I guess there're people out there probably could drink fifteen beers in two hours. Lord knows, there were a few of them there lasst Ssunday."

"Yeah, I know, but it can get kinda' rowdy. Last time I went, there was a fight."

"Lota' sstrange people. Lota' girls coming in by themsselves. I must be getting old. I couldn't believe it, Jerôme. They came in barefoot and wearing ssweatshirtss and bikinis, and I thought I would die. These things were unheard of in my generation. Ssome of the fella's were just plain drunk and rude."

"That's what I mean."

"There was one girl...didn't look to be over nineteen, although I know she would have to be twenty-one to even get in. She was wearing a bikini, sitting at the bar, ssur-rounded by four loud fella's. Didn't sseem to mind their loudness."

"Showing off?"

"Really showing off! All of a ssudden thiss one fel-low reached over and grabbed her bikini top right between her breasstss. He pulled it out and poured beer down the middle, and it got all over her stomach and ran down the front and onto her lap. My lord! I got so embarrassed just watching, but it didn't sseem to bother her or the other fel-la's around her, because they all laughed. They were having a good time. I thought it was pretty dissgussting. I finished my beer and left."

"That's exactly how fights get started," I say. "If one of the other three guys'd got pissed off, you'd've seen a free-for-all. Might've been right in the middle of it, and you'd probably been the one who got hurt, and the four assholes who caused it would've walked out the door."

"I certainly can ssee how that could happen. The bar *was* overcrowded. Actually, that's the ssecond reason I left when I did. Between the jukebox and all those people, I was getting a headache. Not to mention the cigarette smoke."

I've killed off my first beer, so I reach in the bag and grab another.

"Want another beer, Bernie?"

"Still got a half a bottle, thanks."

"Suit yourself. I'm having another one," I say, taking the church key and popping the top off.

It's almost five o'clock. I finish cutting Jorge's hair. Turning him to face the mirror, I say,

"How's that look, Jorge?"

"Can I ssee the back?"

"Sure."

I take the hand mirror and hold it up so he can see the back of his head. He examines it, turning his head from left to right.

"Lookss good," he says.

"Should last you another thousand miles," I say.

I dust the loose hairs from the back of his neck and take off the haircloth.

"You mind if I hang around and finish my beer?" he says after he's paid.

"Go right ahead," I say. "It's go'n'a take us another twenty minutes before we'll get outa' here."

And that's it. So, I start to wipe off my tools and put them away. Bernie's been finished for a few minutes and he's already counting the money in the register.

98

One And Two Halves

"I've got a dinner engagement, sso I've got'a sscoot," Jorge says as he kills off the last of his beer. "I'll ssee you in two weeks."

He goes swinging out the front door. I look around the shop. The lights are out, everybody's gone but me and Bernie, and the shop is quiet and peaceful. Everything's squared away around my chair. I look at my book for tomorrow and can see I've only got two openings left. Bernie's booked up. The phone was kinda' quiet this afternoon. Only that one call from Mike. I'm finishing my beer and waiting for Bernie to figure out how much I made this week, which includes last Saturday's take. I got'a use the restroom so I head back that way. When I come back out, Bernie's sitting in his chair with his jacket on, killing off his beer. He's staring blankly out the front window.

"You ready to split?" I say.

"No hurry. We can relax and finish our beers."

"We did have a hell of a busy day, didn't we?"

"Sure did. You did eight cuts and I did fifteen."

"Well, I've got'a split," I say, as I toss my bottle into the trash. "I'm go'n'a meet Randall and his wife across the street."

"Was that that swell looking tomato that was in here a couple hours ago talking to the guy in your chair?"

"That's the one. Wasn't she fine?"

"I'll say!"

"I'm outa' here. See yuh in the morning."

"Okay. See yuh then."

A couple minutes later I walk into the blaring juke and darkness of the Acapulco Inn, keeping my eyes wide for Randall and Pat.

Bernie

I was alone at the counter of the deli. on the corner, staring out the front window at the college crowd wearing cut-off jeans and sandals. I thought how nice it would be to go over to Trisha's, but I couldn't. As Ann set my lox and bagels on the counter in front of me, I saw Red pass by heading toward the shop. I hadn't been gone five minutes. He was just go'n'a have to wait until I got through eating. I wasn't about to rush back on his account. He shouldn't't've come so early for his appointment. But then it was my bad luck he wouldn't wait for me in the shop. I'd hardly started eating my lunch when he sat down on the stool next to me. Damn! Jerôme probably told him where I was.

"Wha'cha doin' havin' lunch? You're not supposed to take time off to eat." Even though he was saying it like he was kidding, I do believe he was really serious. "I thought I'd come over here and bug ye're ass."

"How you doin', Red?" I said, resigned that I couldn't escape.

"Good. I'll have a cup of coffee," he said to Ann as she stood in front of him with her pad ready. "How's about yourself?"

"Not bad," I said.

I should've gone over to Trisha's for the nooner she wanted. It certainly would've beat the shit out of sitting here with Red. I didn't feel like spending my break talking to him. There'd be another half hour with him after lunch, and

One And Two Halves

that'd be enough. I ate, he drank his coffee, and we sat there for the next fifteen minutes without really saying anything. When I finished, I paid the tab for my lunch and his coffee, and we walked together back to the shop.

*   *   *

Red (his name was Steve Blunt) came in every other week around closing time, usually on a Tuesday or Wednesday, but that week he made his appointment earlier in the day on Friday. He was a nice enough guy, but sometimes he got on my nerves. He'd been hanging around the Shore for many years. His folks came to California from Oklahoma during the Depression. According to the old man, they tried to make a go of it in the fields for a while and gave up because there were too many workers and not enough work. They were having a hell of a time scraping enough together just to eat, so they moved to Long Beach.

The old man took a job as a laborer at the shipyard down at Terminal Island during the war. Red went to all the local schools: Lowell, Rogers and Wilson. By the time he got to Wilson High, he was one of the wildest kids in school. He drove around the Shore in an old Chevy Sedan Delivery with a mattress in back. He really talked a good ladies'-man line, but I think that was a lota' hooie. I think he was one of those guys who talked the loudest and got the least. I used to see him cruising around in that panel wagon, but I don't remember ever seeing a girl with him. I couldn't imagine any gal with any brains or looks wanting to be seen with Red. He finally married a dumpy little, bow-legged gal who wore tight Levi jeans and western-cut shirts with pearl snap-buttons. She looked like a real rodeo queen. In fact, she

101

looked and talked a lot like him, only she wasn't as loud. They were a real redneck couple.

He was always in trouble in high school. He finally got one of those legal ultimatums from a judge where you either join the Army or go to jail. So, he was gone for a couple years, but he still came home on leave and got in trouble again. I think he might've got a bad discharge from the Army.

I used to leave twenty-five dollars in change in the register overnight, and one night someone broke in through the restroom window and robbed me. I was sure it was Red who did it, but I couldn't prove it, so I didn't do anything about it. The reason I thought it was Red was because he'd been my last haircut of the day that afternoon, and he hung around drinking beer with us until I locked the door. I thought he was casing the shop after the second time he'd gone back to use the restroom.

I shampooed his hair and started cutting it. I was moving right along with it when Red said,

"Hey, Bernie, I heard a good joke the other day. Wan'a hear it?"

"Okay," I said, reluctantly.

"There's this piano player goes into a bar lookin' for a job at the piano bar. He sits down at the piano and starts playing for the bar manager. He plays this beautiful tune, and when he finishes, the manager says,

"'Wow! That was a great tune. I don't recognize it. What's it called?'

"Guy says, 'It's one a' my own compositions. I wrote it.'

"Manager says, 'what's the title?'

102

One And Two Halves

"Piano player says, 'I Love You so Fuckin' Much I Could Shit.'

"So, the manager says, 'My God, man. What a bad title for such a beautiful tune. Okay, you got the job, but all you can do is play the piano and entertain the customers. I don't want you talkin' to 'em at all. Not a word. Yuh hear me?'

"Piano player says, 'Okay.'

"His first night on the job, he's playin' when this beautiful chick comes in and sits down at his piano bar and starts comin' on to 'im. So, he's sittin' there playin' and gettin' a hard-on, not sayin' a thing. When he finishes one a' his songs, he can't take no more, so he gets up off his stool and goes into the john to jack off. He comes back out and the dish is still sittin' at his piano bar waitin' for him. She says,

"'Yuh know your fly's unzipped and yuh got come on your pants?'

"'Know it?' he says. 'I wrote it!'"

Then Red started laughing his ass off.

Jerôme and I both had customers in the chair, but things were otherwise quiet in the shop. I wasn't making any effort to talk to Red. A real good-looking young gal wearin' a bikini top and cut-off jeans walked by the front window. Red saw her reflection in the mirror, took his foot off of the footrest and kicked the chair around so he was looking right at her. As she passed the open door, he whistled. It was embarrassing. He tried to get up and go to the door, but I put my hands on his shoulders, restraining him.

I finished drying his hair and started working on the taper and the sideburns. His sideburns were out of proportion with the length of his hair, but he liked them that way so I didn't bother raising them. Instead, I squared them to a pointed boot running along his jawbone which was probably an inch or so longer than the length on the nape. One more thing that showed what a redneck he was.

"Hey Bernie, ever hear the one about the dumb bartender?"

"I don't know."

That's all I said, hoping he'd forget it and not tell me the joke.

"Well, it goes like this. Yuh see there's this dumb bartender, and five chicks sittin' at the bar. This guy comes in off the street and stands back and looks up and down at the girls and then walks over and orders a drink. As he's sippin' on his drink, he turns to the gal next to him and says, real quiet like. So quiet she can't hardly hear him,

"'Tickle your ass with a feather?'

"She turns on him all put out and says,

"'I beg your pardon?'

"He c'n see she's all pissed off, so he says louder,

"'Particularly nasty weather,' and she says,

"'Oh.'"

Just about that time, Red's wife walked in the shop with their son, and having heard what he'd just said, she said,

"Tellin' 'im the one 'bout the dumb bartender?"

"Yeah," he said, and she and the little boy started laughing. "So anyways, this guy moves down the bar to the next good-looking chick and says,

"'Tickle your ass with a feather?' and she gets all pissed off like the first one and says,

"'What?' and he says,

"'Particularly nasty weather,' and she says,

"'Oh.'

One And Two Halves

"Well, this guy goes all the way down the bar tellin' every single chick in there the same thing until one of 'em says,

"'Sounds like fun. Let's do it.'

"So they leave together. Well, this dumb bartender's been watching this, and he wonders how the guy does it, so he decides to ask the guy the next time he sees 'im. So, when the guy comes back, he starts doin' it all over again, and the bartender takes him to one side and says,

"'Duh, I saw yuh pick up a chick in here the other day, and I was wonderin' what the hell you're sayin' to 'em.'

"'It's easy,' the guy says. 'All yuh got'a do is walk up to a gal and say,

"'"Tickle your ass with a feather?"' and if she's not game, all yuh got'a say is,

"'"Particularly nasty weather,"' and then you're off the hook. If she likes what she hears, then yuh got it made."

"'"I get it,"' the bartender says.

"So, he goes up to one of the chicks at the bar and tries it out:

"He says, 'duh, stick a feather up ye're ass?' and naturally she gets all pissed off and says,

"'"What did you say?"' and he says,

"'"Look at the fuckin' rain."'"

When he hit the punch line, all three of them, Red, his wife and their kid, were almost rolling on the floor. Herb White had come in in the middle of Red's joke, and he was laughing too, but not nearly as much as they were.

I was finished with the haircut, so I showed him the back and he got out of the chair. Standing next to his wife and kid, he looked like her, and their kid looked like a miniature of both of them. All three of them walked out of the shop on bowlegs, and Herb sat down in my chair, ready for his haircut.

*   *   *

Herb was a young guy who wore his hair in a flattop. He started coming in the shop before appointments and hairstyling. J.D. was working the second chair at the time. It must've been five years before that Good Friday. I got the feeling he'd be a one-time customer who wouldn't come back a second time, but he did. J.D. only cut his hair a couple times and then he died, and that's when Herb came to me. He never got in Jerôme's chair. For some reason he liked us older barbers. He said he wanted his flattop cut so he could balance a book on it, but the problem was the top of his head was shaped like a church steeple.

I shampooed and towel-dried his short hair and was cutting the sides with the number two blade when he pulled his head away slowly and looked at me. I shut the clippers off and in a hushed voice, he said,

"Bernie, I wonder, uh, wha'da yuh think about a woman steppin' out on her husband? I mean, what would you do if you found out your wife was steppin' out on you?"

This was another one of those situations where a customer'll tell his barber things he'd never tell anybody else. I turned Herb around so he was facing me. I lowered my voice and said,

"What happened? You find out yer wife's been playing around on the sly?"

"Possible. Don't know for sure. Always thought she was true to me. I mean, I'm not such a bad guy. I have a good job, I come home after work, and I don't mess around behind *her* back."

"Yuh never know why women do some of the stuff they do. What makes yuh think she's cheatin'?"

"Take a look at this letter I found yesterday in the nightstand next to the bed."

He pulled a pink piece of paper from his wallet, unfolded it and gave it to me. I lit a cigarette and looked over the piece of paper. At the bottom of the page, there were some flowers and written under them were the words, "I wonder if these flowers go at the top of the letter." Then I started reading:

"Easley,

I was delighted to hear of your unfaithful adventures; that makes us twins. But I'm planning on being faithful from now on. Roger and Jack came and visited me in Goleta (and Jacks cousin, there was something about her appearance that bothered me. but I couldn't quite put my finger on it so I let it slide.) They invited me to go with them to Rogers cabin, so I said sure. It was about a week after I got there (Goleta) and I was feeling mad because Bruce wasn't sorry he hit me so I went to get my revenge. Anyway, how can you expect me to resist such a marvelous quacker as Jackson (His cousins looks still made me fidget, but I couldn't figure out exactly what it was.) Poor old Jackson drank too much and passed out. That night, while lying awake in my bed feeling rotten about cheating on Bruce, It struck me what it was about Jacks cousin (I can't remember her name) that bothered me. She looks like Bruce's mother. Needless to say, she's no beauty. She's also weird and poor Roger was sorry he got stuck with her. I missed you terribly

107

then (I sound like your love) because I didn't have anyone to tell my sin to. When I got back to Hemet, I told Bruce and he wasn't even mad, he was very understanding, but it all seemed so simple; I think there must be a catch somewhere. Anyway, I've stayed faithful almost a week now. I saw Tom Jones. *WOW*. He has got to be the most sexiest male alive. He does something to you physically.

"My daddy keeps inquiring about you. He can't seem to remember that one of his daughters is in Europe.

"You must write to me and tell me every thing you do. Write smaller and you can fit more on. When you come home, I'd be more than willing to meet you at the airport. I miss you more than I miss Bruce. Your husband will probably make you stay home a few days, but then we can go to Santa Barbara for as long as you want.

"It's not that my handwriting is bad, it's just that there aren't any lines on the paper.

"This whole letter is filled with nothing but what I have been doing; so I will expect the same from you. I am expecting a detailed account. Do not disappoint me.

"Have a wonderful time and don't worry about anything or anybody. Such an opportunity as the one your taking comes once in a life time.

"Writing letters isn't bad at all, I think I'm going to write you some more.

Love,

Sonya"

"Your wife got this in the mail?" I asked, handing the letter back to him.

108

One And Two Halves

I turned the clipper on and tapered up the back still using the number two. When I'd gotten around to the other side, I took the number two off and snapped the one-and-a-half on to get the lower sides and back.

"Yes. Sonya's her friend who lives out on the desert. Year before last we decided in earnest that we were going to have children, so Easley went to Europe with Sonya's sister and spent about a month there before we got started. One more trip before having a baby. Yuh know, we'd been trying for a couple years with no luck.

"This letter makes it sound like my wife had an affair while she was traveling over there, but I can't be sure because Sonya doesn't really spell it out. *She* probably doesn't know anything either."

"There isn't a whole hell of a lot you can do about it now, is there? And really at this point, what difference does it make? He's over there and she's over here. They can't be carrying on an affair five thousand miles apart, can they? I think you ought'a just forget it."

"But I can't."

By then he was fretting. I was looking at his tormented face in the mirror on the opposite wall as I flattened out the top of his pointed head.

"I'm go'n'a confront her with this letter and see what she has to say. I've made up my mind."

As far as I was concerned, that would've been a mistake, but I kept quiet. I knew that anything I said, he wouldn't want to hear anyway.

"Suit yourself," I said.

"I've got to do it. You see we had a baby girl only eight months after she got home, and the baby wasn't premature. Like I said before, we'd been trying for three years with no results, and eight months after she got back from a month's vacation in Europe, she had a seven-pound six-ounce baby. I'm no mathematician, but I can add, and it sure seems fishy to me. I wan'a find out if that baby's mine or some European gigolo's."

I was knocking the corners down with my Wahl clippers, and generally smoothing up the edges. Then I took my Outliner and squared off the sideburns and sharpened up the arch over the ears and the lines down the back of the neck.

Herb's flattop was so easy that I was ahead of schedule, so I was looking forward to another cigarette break and a look at the college girls in bikinis out on the sidewalk. I showed him the sides and back in the hand mirror and got his approval. Then he got out of the chair, paid for the haircut and left.

When I went back to my chair to sweep up, I saw the letter lying in the hair on the floor, so I picked it up and headed out the door to give it back to him, but he had disappeared into the crowd on Second Street. I turned and went back into the shop and put the letter on top of the radio for when he came back to get it. That letter sat there for a couple weeks before I threw it away, and I never saw Herb again.

*   *   *

I lit another cigarette and sat down in the chair in the front window. I smoked and watched the bustle of the crowd on the sidewalk and the traffic in the street. Then I got up and checked my book again to see who was due in next. It was Bill Donovan, the used car salesman. His would be another easy haircut. I always had a good time cutting his hair, and he usually gave me a good tip, too. I sat down in the chair by the window, but no sooner did I do it than Bill walked in, so I got up and went over and stood by my chair.

"How yuh doin', Bill?" I said as he rummaged through the magazines on the table by the cash register.

"Fine," he said, picking up the *Saturday Evening Post.*

He sat in the chair and closed his eyes as I put him back in the sink. The magazine was opened, face down and spread out on his stomach. After the shampoo I put him back upright, and he started reading. As I was topping his hair, I could see over his shoulder that he was reading an article in the *Post* about a big political scandal in Massachusetts. Every once in a while, he'd snicker and shake his head. When he did, I'd have to stop what I was doing and steady him so I could continue.

"What're yuh reading there, Bill?

"An article about corruption in Boston. Politics and politicians're really something else. They play these games with millions of dollars and millions of people's lives without batting an eye.

"This story's about an eight-million-dollar payoff to a politician so he'll vote for a bill to build a parking structure in downtown Boston. Yuh know how much eight million dollars is? I sold a Chevy last week for two thousand. For me that's a big deal. Some people're havin' a hard-enough time just scraping rent together. That's reality. Politicians're living in a different world. This jerk in the White House is a classic example. I wonder who he thinks he's kidding. Just another rich guy who cashed in at the taxpayers' expense. How'n hell is he go'n'a pay for this war over in Vietnam.

111

Some more taxpayers' money. It's crazy, but it's politics, and they don't get why we're so pissed off.

"And then Johnson declares war on poverty and disease too, and then just because he makes the declaration, he thinks it'll just go away. He ought'a declare a war on war, and maybe then Vietnam'll go away."

"You're preachin' to the choir here. I think Johnson's a wastrel."

"My wife's a schoolteacher in a real tough area in Los Angeles. Mostly Mexicans and Colored. These kids are so poor they don't even have lunch money most days. But you know what? As deprived as they are, their parents take a real interest in their education, and the kids themselves actually like going to school. It takes their minds off their hard times, and the parents see education as a way out of hard times for their kids. The parents come to the open houses and parent conferences, and they want to know what they can do to help with their kids's educations.

"Before she got transferred, Suzie was teachin' in Hancock Park. She likes where she is now a hell of a lot better. The rich kids really didn't give a damn about school, and they were spoiled rotten. Their parents'd pull 'em out and take 'em to Colorado in the ski season. The sixth graders had their own motor scooters. When they studied Europe, they were bored 'cause they'd been to Europe at least once, some of 'em twice. Those kids had more pocket change than I have. Difference between them and the ones she's got now is night and day. The rich kids's parents were a much bigger pain in the ass than the poor kids's parents. They were always hangin' around, gettin' in Suzie's way, tryin' to tell her how to teach, and what the hell did they know about it? Nothing!

112

One And Two Halves

"I've asked myself who's really deprived, the rich kids or the poor kids. Sure, the poor kids have it rough, but they have better survival instincts. Later when they grow up, who'll be better equipped to cut it in the real world? I think the poor kids. True, rich kids do have the money, and that's a big advantage, but the poor kids have a better understanding of reality. It's just like this magazine article. You and I are the ones who're living with reality. Those millionaire politicians don't have a clue."

"I couldn't agree more, but it hasn't changed up to now, and I don't think it's go'n'a change real soon."

"Right. I can't help laughing at it. If you don't laugh, you'll go crazy. That's why I smile and shake my head when I read stuff like this."

As I was toweling off his hair, my mind wandered. I thought about Trisha again, how it would've been nice to see her, but there was no way, so I started thinking of ways to get over there the following week. The floor was looking pretty bad. That'd be my excuse to get down here. I could come down Monday, clean up real quick and then go over to Trisha's and spend a couple hours with her. I was getting a hard-on just thinking about it.

After I got Donovan's hair dry, I did shears over comb up the back and on the sides until it was blended with the top. Then I took my Wahls and tapered the sideburns and nape until they were blended with the shear work. I squared the sideburns with the Outliner and cleaned up the fuzz on the base of his neck. It was looking smooth and even all over so I checked it in the mirror to make sure there were no lines in it. It was looking good to me. I showed him the back in the hand mirror. I knew he wouldn't have any complaints, and he didn't.

113

"Looks good as usual, Bernie. My hair's never looked as good as it has since you've been cutting it."

"Know what I say to that. Tell a friend."

"I tell all my friends. Don't worry about that. What's the damage?"

"Five bucks."

"There you go," he said, handing me a sawbuck. "You got four ones?"

"Sure," I said, ringing it up on the register.

I took out the four singles and gave them to him. He thanked me and took his place with the crowd on the sidewalk where the midday sun left no shade on either side of Second Street.

*   *   *

I was folding my haircloth to lay it over the arm of my chair, when Doc came in. Jerôme cut his hair once, but Doc told me he didn't like the haircut, so he came to me from then on. Doc was a little guy with thinning gray hair, and he had a nose like Jimmy Durante's, only more prominent because of the pockmarks from the acne he'd obviously had when he was a kid. He'd probably picked the pimples, and that's why it was so scarred.

He liked to be called "Doc," but he wasn't a doctor; he was a cosmetics salesman. His name was Joe Ferguson. He told me he was a medical school drop-out in Washington state, but the story I heard was that he'd only gotten through two years of junior college, and he never even got the college degree in chemistry he told everybody he had, much less went to medical school.

114

One And Two Halves

He sat down in my chair grumbling as usual and not being very sociable. He warned me to be real careful cutting the hair in his ears. He said he had an infection and to not stick my shears in too far. It was against the state barber law to insert your shears into anybody's ears or nose anyway. He said if I did stick them in there, he wanted to make sure I sterilized them real good. It was also against the state barber law not to sterilize your tools before you used them, so I made sure he saw me sterilize them.

"Well, Bernie," he said, "how 'bout them Angels?"

I wasn't much of a baseball fan. Asa was the baseball fan around there; Jerôme was the football fan; the only sport I cared about was thoroughbred horse racing. So I said to him,

"I don't know. What about 'em?"

"They're playin' their first season in their new ballpark down in Anaheim. It's go'n'a be real swell to have major league baseball closer to home."

"I guess."

I didn't know what he was talking about, and I didn't care, either.

"They got some good material this year, too," Doc said. "They should be pretty good, but Dodgers're go'n'a be better."

"Oh, yeah?"

"Dodgers've got Koufax and Drysdale, and they're real tough this year. They've got the makings of a great team. They could go all the way."

Since I wasn't interested in what he wanted to talk about, I didn't say anything, and his chatter tapered off into silence for a little while. I set him back up in the chair and toweled his hair, getting it ready to cut. I combed it straight

115

back and parted it. Then I combed the sides down over the tops of his ears. The taper on his neck was still in pretty good shape except it was getting a little shaggy along the bottom. I picked up my shears and started topping it.

"Yeah, the Angels might have a pretty good ball team this year," he said. "They just bought this college boy Reichardt who was an all-American at Wisconsin in both football and baseball. That'll help 'em a lot, but they've got'a do some more building before they'll be any good. I think this spring training was just a fluke. They've only been in the league a few years and they're doing a pretty good job. Their second year in business, they finished third after being in first on the fourth of July, but they ain't got the stars like Koufax and Drysdale and them Davis boys too, and how about Howard and Roseboro? The Angels just ain't got stars like that. I'll tell yuh it's go'n'a be nice to go to a game in Anaheim, and not have to go into that jungle up in L.A."

"I suppose you'll be an Angel fan when they move down here, huh?" I said.

"I'll always be a Dodger fan. I was a Dodger fan when they were still in Brooklyn. Once a Dodger fan, always a Dodger fan, but I'll go to the Angels games since it'll be so close. Angels've some good ball players like Fregosi and Cardenal; they're just not as good as the Dodgers."

"Don't you root for the underdog?"

"Sure, when they have a chance to do something. Like the Dodgers, for instance. Every year comes around, and everybody says what a buncha' bums they are, and every year Koufax and Drysdale win over twenty games and Koufax has an earned run average of below two point oh. Now those are the kind of underdogs I like to root for. Nobody ever gives 'em an outside chance, but every year they prove how good they are."

"How can they be underdogs? Seems like they're in the World Series every year. And don't they fill the ballpark every game? That's like calling Willie Shoemaker an underdog."

"They brought the championship to L.A.," he said, sounding a tad belligerent. "That's more'n the Angels ever did, and it looks like they're go'n'a do it again this year. Hell, they may be as good as those old Yankee clubs of the fifties. You couldn't beat some a' them old Yankee teams with Ford and Berra, Skowron, Richardson, and Boyer, and then there was Mantle, too. They just don't make teams like that anymore, except the Dodgers."

I didn't understand what he was talking about. He said the Dodgers were underdogs, but then he admitted they were a championship team. He said everybody called the Dodgers bums, but then agreed they always had a full stadium. None of it made sense to me.

"To tell the truth," he said, "I don't follow the American League real close. Once a Dodger fan, always a National League fan."

"Oh," I said.

Stew, my next cut, staggered in and sat down in the waiting chair in the front window. He was already drunk, and it wasn't even three o'clock.

"How's it goin', Stew?" I said.

"Pre' goo', Bern. How's 'bout se'f?"

"Good."

I started tapering the sides and back of Doc's hair. He said something, but my mind was wandering and I didn't hear it, so I just ignored him and picked up my pace so I

117

could get rid of him faster. I was tired of listening to him. I wasn't interested in the things he wanted to talk about.

After I finished the cut, I dusted off his nape and showed him the back of his head in the hand mirror. He said it looked okay, so I unsnapped the haircloth and took it off. He gave me five dollars even and stood there waiting like he expected some change.

"That's it, Doc," I said. "Five bucks even. Have a nice Easter. See yuh later."

"Oh, okay," he said shaking his head, looking bewildered. "See yuh later, Bernie. Don't bet against the Dodgers this year."

"I won't. Don't worry," I said, and he disappeared out the door. What a cheap bastard he was. I gave him all that conversation and he didn't even give me a tip.

*   *   *

I went to my chair and dusted it off. Then I poked Stew on the knee and told him to come over and have a seat. He woke up with a shake of his head. He stood up, went to the chair and sat down. It was pretty obvious he'd been down at O'Shea's since opening time. He got off work around then because it was Good Friday. His nose was red, and his vacant eyes were bloodshot. He wound up sleeping through that haircut, which wasn't unusual. He slept through most of 'em 'cause any time he got one, he was usually half stiff.

I never saw a guy get through the day quicker'n Stew. His name was well suited to him. I never heard anybody call him by his first name. I think the guys down at O'Shea's nicknamed him with the first part of his last name just because they rarely ever saw him sober. Stew was a thirty-grand-a-year middle management exec. at Douglas Aircraft out on Lakewood Boulevard. He'd talked about how his management buddies in the office made passes at the young, good lookin' secretaries, and how the junior-executive-Joe-college types thought they were someday go'n'a be president of the company. He made it sound like the only real people out there were the workers in the shops because all you had to do was hand them a rivet gun or a wrench and that kept them happy.

That was the business side of Stew. His personal life was just as screwed up. He'd been married and divorced three times, and his second wife took him for everything he had at the time. He'd owned a used car lot on Vermont up in Los Angeles. He wasn't getting rich, but he was making a comfortable living. It was right after the war, and the car business was just starting to move. He didn't have any kids, so he and his wife lived in a small mansion in the Hollywood hills, and he sported around in a Caddy.

The salesman who worked for him was the one who screwed everything up. The guy would take his lunch hour, leaving Stew to mind the store, and he'd go over to Stew's house and get a little afternoon delight off Stew's wife. That was going on for who knows how long, and Stew wasn't catching on. One day out of the blue, she sued him for divorce and got everything—the house, the car, the business and fifty a month alimony. She didn't get child support only because they didn't have any kids. In fact, Stew never had any kids out of all three wives.

As soon as she took over the car business, the first thing she did was fire Stew. She must've had a guilty conscience and didn't want to have to look him in the face. She

119

did keep her boyfriend working there though, and Stew was out on his ass with nothing to his name but the clothes on his back. He went back to his first wife who was hustling in the bars downtown. She put him up until he could get back on his feet, which he did by getting a job at Douglas.

In the meantime, the used car salesman must've got tired of Stew's second wife because he made a cash deal one day, closed up the lot and took off with the dough. It only took her six months to lose the whole works. She couldn't get anybody she could rely on to run the lot, so she lost it within three months; then she lost the Caddy; and finally the house went. Stew said he never saw her after that.

He worked his way from a sales position up the ladder to a management spot at Douglas, going through another marriage in the process. He was now a bachelor, and he swore he'd stay that way.

"I hope somebody puts a gun to my head if I ever mention getting married again," I once heard him say.

Stew's head nodded forward, and I pulled it back with my left hand.

Activity on the street was just over the peak, so it was still very crowded. The sun bathers were out in force, but it wouldn't be too long before they'd be thinning, heading home to get dressed for the night's activities. There were parties all over the Shore that night. I was glad to be getting close to the end of my day. I wanted to get the hell out of there and go home.

Just then a tall, beautiful woman came in and stood next to Jerôme's chair. She talked for a couple minutes with Jerôme's customer, and then she got up and walked back out onto the street. I stopped what I was doing and watched her leave. She was the best-looking thing I'd seen all day.

120

One And Two Halves

The afternoon wend- ed its way toward the end. The sun was still fairly high, but the sidewalks on my side of the street were just starting to be in shade. The street and sidewalk on the other side of the street were still sunny. The orange sign above the door of the Acapulco Inn was a little brighter than before as the sun dropped in the sky. On Second Street the bathing suits and cutoff Levis were still the style. The numbers were the same, and so were the faces. I'd been working on their hair all day—in fact, all my life, and I'd be working on them all the rest of my life. One of them was sleeping in my chair while I was trying to hold his head still and cut his hair at the same time.

When I finished topping, I towel-dried the sides and back and started working there with the shears. Then I cleaned up the neckline and sideburns with the Osters. I used the Wahls for the finish. I wiped off the back of Stew's neck with the damp towel and undid the haircloth. After looking at the job in the mirror, I was satisfied, but that really didn't matter. It was good enough for Stew. In his condition he wouldn't recognize a mistake if he saw one. I shook his shoulder.

"Wake up, Stew. I'm all done."

I was holding the hand mirror up for him, but he was half asleep, nodding his head and snorting.

"Wake up, Stew," I repeated.

"Huh, oh, uh, yeah. All done, huh?"

He rolled his head and stepped out of the chair brushing the hand mirror aside as he staggered past me. He took a wallet out of his hip pocket, handed me a ten-dollar bill. He turned and went out the door before I could say thanks or offer him change.

121

Jerome Arthur

I watched him cross the street and stumble into the Acapulco Inn. I put the sawbuck in the register and took out a five and stuck it in my pocket. Then I cleaned up around my chair, wiped off the countertop on the backbar and cleaned up my tools. I brushed off my clippers and oiled them. After I hung them up, I sat down and lit a cigarette.

*   *   *

I looked at my chair and took a deep breath. I got caught up on my schedule with Stew so I had a couple minutes before my next customer was due to come in. I hadn't swept the floor, and I stood there in the hair, smoking and staring at Jerôme as he worked on his customer. I came out of it and went back and got the broom, leaving my cigarette in the ashtray on my backbar. When I finished sweeping, I took a couple more drags and splashed my face with cool water. It sure felt good.

It must've been up in the mid-seventies that day because I was feeling warm, and everybody out on the street was dressed light. I imagined it was pretty wild down at the beach. Drunk college boys raisin' hell. I was sure Jerôme wanted to be there rather than here in the shop. No thanks, I'd rather be cutting hair and makin' some dough. I was always glad to be making money, and having the crowd come to me.

After I dried my face and hands, I put my glasses back on and combed through the few strands of hair on top and flattened out the sides. When I finished doing that, Garrett Tilson, the teacher, walked through the front door and went over and picked up the newspaper. He turned and walked back to my chair and sat down.

One And Two Halves

He was originally a walk-in, and he'd been coming to me ever since. I didn't have a thing in common with him, and he was never happy with his haircut. That is, he always told me to do something else when I was through with him. I had a lot of cuts like that that day. Clint, Larry, Red. Teach should have gotten into Jerôme's chair. He was young like Jerôme, and he might've had more to talk about with him.

"Did you see that program on T.V. last night about Moby Dick?" he asked.

"No," I answered. "What was it about?"

"Well, are you familiar with *Moby Dick,* the book by Melville?"

"I never read it, but I've heard about it," I said.

"Well, let me tell you about the program. It was on channel two, narrated by Charles Kuralt and George C. Scott. It started out with the sound of seagulls and the rushing of the surf. Scott started the narration, with 'Call me Ishmael.' That's the first line of the novel. Then Kuralt segued in, discussing some of the ancient mysteries of the sea."

I didn't know for sure who any of those people were, actors and T.V. personalities, I guessed. He talked as I cut, and every now and then, I'd say something like, "Oh," or "Uh huh."

"After the introduction, they had a commercial. You know, it's really amazing how they make the commercials coincide with the subject matter of the T.V. program. Being a junior high English teacher, it really adds to the continuity of the subject matter. A work of art is created in its totality. Commercials don't necessarily have to detract from it.

"Well, this commercial was about Polaroid cameras. A man was sitting on the gunwale of his sloop, and he was

123

talking about the Polaroid Swinger. Right behind him is the most beautiful blond girl. He's explaining the different features of the camera, and then he turns to take a picture of the girl. She sure was pretty."

I looked at his reflection in the mirror and he was actually blushing. Then I overheard Jerôme talking to his customer, telling him how he planned to keep cutting hair after he got his degree, and his customer telling him that he should get a better job with his education. That's when I said,

"I been tryin' to tell 'im he should do something with his education, but he ain't listenin' to me."

Without missing a beat, Garrett picked up his story about the T.V. show he'd seen the night before.

"Then the next commercial was that one for Winston cigarettes. You know the one with the girl in a kilt, dancing to bagpipes? She sang, 'It's what's up front that counts.' Then the last two ads were about Sucrets. The first one was about a young boy gargling with Sucrets mouthwash, and it was so realistic that they had the mouthwash splashing from his mouth onto the camera lens. The second one was about a man with a cough taking Sucrets lozenges. It was realistic too because when he coughed, the camera lens fogged up.

"When they got back to the program, the T.V. people were interviewing some fishermen in Nantucket getting ready to go to sea. Scott was quoting some more from *Moby Dick* and Kuralt was talking to the sailors in the background.

"'And thus have these naked Nantucketers, these sea hermits, issuing from their ant-hill in the sea, overrun and conquer the watery world like so many Alexanders....'

"Then the sailors could be heard saying things like, 'man is the biggest destroyer on earth.' Did you know they're the only ones in the animal kingdom who hunt for sport and not for food for their families?"

"I guess I heard that."

"The next scene was on board this ship, the *Seattle*. The sailors were talking about the upcoming halibut season and George C. Scott was dropping in alternate comments about the whale hunt. Is the halibut a big fish?" he asked interrupting himself.

"Huh? Oh, I'm not sure. I'm not much of a fisherman. How come you ask?"

"Oh, I was just wondering if the T.V. people were trying to present a subtle type of irony. It just seems to me that if they were going to do a parody of *Moby Dick*, they should use a fish equally as impressive as a whale to do it. Something similar to their using commercials that correspond with the material on the program. Do you see the picture I'm trying to paint?"

"Oh yeah," I answered.

I didn't know what the hell he was talking about. Then I looked over at Jerôme. He would normally have something to say about this kind of conversation, but he was busy talking to the guy in his own chair. Then Teach started up again.

"It was real strange how when the T.V. people interviewed the sailors individually, they said they didn't really know what they were doing. They were merely following orders.

"Then a Japanese freighter pulled alongside the *Seattle*. You should have heard some of the comments the sailors were making, things like,

"'A real jap ship,' and among the laughs, 'Lack a' nooky.'

Jerome Arthur

"I was surprised that these kinds of racist comments got by the censors. Then, worst of all, the American sailors passed the Japanese sailors a copy of *Playboy*. The only saving grace of that magazine is those clever advertisements that it has. I have to tell you that I was shocked, but they switched scenes quickly.

"The next thing you knew, you saw a whale. I don't know if it was a sperm whale, white whale or what. But the myriad sailors' voices could be heard saying,

"'Moby Dick! Yes, it's Moby Dick!'

"Then it was time for another commercial. This time they advertised Winston cigarettes, Polaroid cameras and R.C.A. television sets. The Winston commercial this time was that one where they have a group of people surfing in an outrigger in Hawaii. They sing a jingle that goes, 'It's not how long you make it, it's how you make it long.' And all of the actors are moving the words around on the screen.

"The Polaroid ad was a very touching one. It showed a young boy with his dog running in slow motion through wheat that was as tall as the boy himself. The caption said something about not letting the good times go by unremembered. With a Polaroid camera, good times can be kept permanent on film. I know because I have one, and it was the best investment I ever made.

"And of course, I'm sure you're familiar with the most recent R.C.A. commercials, where they have this beautiful Negro girl sitting on top of the T.V. set itself, and she splits in half and shows the various 'smears' that a regular T.V. has, 'smears' that don't appear on an 'R.C.A. non-smear color T.V. set.'

"When the program came back on, the engines of the boat were droning, and Kuralt was interviewing several of

126

the crew members. It really did amaze me how caught up in life, death and immortality those sailors were. Of course, they indicated that they were getting a little impatient to catch some fish, but they were questioning whether God exists, and if He does, whether He's looking out for them. It really did remind me a great deal of Ishmael.

"Then the scene switched to one of the sailors standing on the deck shooting some seals. When he hit one, he'd turn and smile into the camera and bite down on his cigar. They finally caught some fish, and it showed them cleaning them.

"Then it was time for another commercial. Carnation Slender had a cute little skit about a pretty girl sitting at a make-up table telling how she stays beautiful by drinking Carnation Slender. They showed her four children, and I really believe that she didn't look any older than twenty-one or twenty-two.

"The next commercial came back to the *Moby Dick* theme. It was Coffee Mate, and it showed a man come aboard an empty yacht looking for somebody, and all he found was a fresh pot of coffee. He had some coffee with Coffee Mate and then he started talking about how it tasted just like fresh cream. I've used Coffee Mate, and I really do think it's better than fresh cream.

"The last commercial was Colgate toothpaste with M.F.P. fluoride which was very clever. They have this dentist wearing a white jacket, and he's holding a book of statistics that says Colgate with M.F.P. is proven to be more effective against cavities. I tried it and I think it's true.

"The show concluded with beautiful sea sounds: seagulls, breaking surf, etc. and the credits being flashed on the screen. It was really a great show. How did you like it?"

"I didn't see it," I said.

"But I just told you all about it."

"Oh, it was okay."

His haircut was finished, and I was bracing myself for a complaint.

"Hey," he said. "Didn't I tell you not to skin the sides?"

He said it so loud that Jerôme and his customer both looked at him, and then at me. Then he got out of the chair and got about six inches from the mirror and examined every single hair.

"Okay," he said. "Take just a little more off the top on the left side here. I told you I wanted it cut in an ivy-league style, like those guys in the Kingston Trio."

When he said that, suddenly it hit home how he really believed all those T.V. commercials. So, I just hurried up and took off the hair he told me to and tried to get rid of him. He checked the haircut again, got out of the chair and went to the cash register. I followed him, took his money and that was the end of it. He passed Chad, my next cut, as he went out the door.

*   *   *

By the time Chad Moriarty came in, my day was winding down. I'd been taking the customers as they came in, bang, bang, bang, and I was getting a little tired by then. The only thing I was looking forward to was finishing up and going home. Well, that and watching the feature race in a little bit.

Chad went over and talked to Jerôme, and then he came back and sat down in my chair. I looked out the win-

128

One And Two Halves

dow and noticed that our side of the street was completely in shade, and the sun cast a luminous reflection on the orange sign above the door of the Acapulco Inn. I'd cut Chad's hair before, but he wasn't anybody's regular customer. He'd make an appointment with whoever answered the phone, and the instructions were never elaborate. All he wanted was a haircut. He was a young guy from Oklahoma who hung around with Jerôme and his crowd across the street. That bar was probably the first place he went to when he hit town. Not long after his arrival, I'd see him walking up and down the street with different Belmont Shore locals; it hadn't taken him long to make friends here.

"How're yuh doin', Chad?" I asked as he sat down in the chair.

"Fine. How 'bout yourself?"

"Can't complain. How yuh want yer hair cut today?"

"Leave it a little longer this time. Just kind of trim it a little around the ears and back of the neck. I think I want to let the sideburns get a little longer, too. That seems to be the style right now."

"Ye're right. Been saying for a long time that styles are getting longer and they're go'n'a get longer yet."

"Yeah. Even the politicians are letting their sideburns grow out. Elvis was ahead of his time. I saw a picture of Jesse Unruh the other day, and man, his sideburns are all the way down to his jawbone."

"Of course, you know those politicians are go'n'a be doing what's politically expedient, whether it's what they wan'a do 'r not, 'specially one like Big Daddy Unruh. He's nothing but a boss like Daly in Chicago. Goldwater and Reagan are about the only ones around who are honest

129

enough to say what they really think without worrying whether it's politically expedient."

"Ah come on now, Bernie. Those guys're politicians too, and they'll put a sugar coating over a thing if it's to their benefit. They're just like the others."

"I don't agree with that, but that's what makes life interesting, different people with different points of view. When Jerôme first came to work for me, he had liberal leanings, and we used to have some pretty good discussions, but he gradually changed over to my way of thinking when I showed him that the liberals really haven't accomplished much. So now it's actually kind of boring when we discuss politics because he agrees with me so much."

"No kiddin'. So that's where he's been gettin' that right-wing rhetoric he's been talkin' lately. I didn't think it was really him talking."

"You're a conservative, aren't you? Being from Oklahoma and all?"

"Well, I voted for Johnson in sixty-four and I'm go'n'a vote for Brown for governor against Reagan in November. I happen to think we were cheated out of a president when Kennedy got shot; that's why I hope Ted Kennedy runs in 'sixty-eight. I'll vote for him."

"What about Bobby?"

I was beginning to wish I hadn't got into that conversation. I didn't agree with any of this. Chad was a good customer, and I didn't want to antagonize him.

"I don't like Bobby. I liked Jack and I like Ted because he reminds me of Jack. Somehow Bobby seems too ruthless to me, but I'd vote for him if he ever ran. Any Democrat is better than any Republican."

130

One And Two Halves

"'Far as I'm con- cerned, the Democrats're all the same. They say they wan'a help out the poor; only problem is, they want to use my money to do it. Instead of giving yuh the shirt off their own backs, they wan'a give yuh the shirt off my back."

I didn't raise my voice. I was trying to stay calm. He didn't say anything. He just shrugged and sat quiet in the chair.

"It just goes to show how a person can make a mistake about somebody," I said, cooling down a little and smiling. "I thought you were probably a Republican, being educated and prosperous as you seem to be."

"Boy, I wish I was," he said, "prosperous, that is. As far as my education's concerned, I got that as a result of generous Democratic education policies."

I didn't want to get into an argument, so I shut up for a few minutes and concentrated on the haircut. He didn't say anything either. Instead, he kept his eye on me in the mirror on the opposite wall.

"Do you ever read Jim Murray in the *Times*?" he asked, changing the subject.

"Is he an editorialist?"

"No. Well, yeah, he is. He writes a column in the sports section. He's good; you ought'a read 'im sometime. He's funny as hell. He's not what you'd call a traditional sportswriter. He pokes fun at most of the myths about athletes and athletics."

"Oh yeah? About the only part of the sports section I read is the race results, and I get that out of the *Press-Telegram*."

"No kidding? You're a horse race fan, huh?"

131

"Well, not as much as I used to be, but I keep an eye on the ponies. I used to ride 'em when I was younger."

He didn't respond to that, as if he didn't know whether I was talking about racehorses or just horses in general.

"You used to be a jockey?" he finally said, realizing what I'd meant.

"Certainly. Started riding when I was fifteen years old and quit when I was nineteen. That's when I joined the Navy and went off to the war."

"How'd yuh get into barbering?"

"Started learning early. My dad was a barber. When I wasn't riding, I hung around his shop watching him cut hair. Then when I joined the Navy, I was a Ship Serviceman, and that's where I got my practical experience. The Navy also fed me on a regular basis. Spuds three meals a day. I started filling out, and I couldn't do light anymore. By the time I got out, I was too heavy, so my riding days were over. You can see I couldn't be a jockey now. When yuh get out of the chair, take a walk to the back of the shop. Pictures on the wall are me in 'thirty-nine when I was ridin'."

"Saw 'em before; didn't know it was you. I thought it was just some old pictures you had. Know any of the jockeys who're ridin' today?"

"Nah. About the only person connected with racing that I know now is my bookie, and all he does is take my money."

"You ever make a little book yourself?" he asked. "You got a perfect front here."

"Nah. It don't pay. There's too many risks. It's illegal, so there's the constant fear of gettin' arrested. Then there's the problem of paying off a big winner. And if you

132

make it through that, you get jumped and beat up by some hoodlum like what happened to my bookie."

Suddenly it dawned on me that it was getting close to time for the feature race on T.V., and almost at the same time, Asa came around the corner of his door and peeked in mine and said,

"It's a quarter after, Bernard. They'll be starting up pretty soon."

"Am I glad you reminded me," I said. "Until now I forgot all about it. 'Scuse me, Chad, I'm go'n'a set up the T.V. so we can watch the feature race."

"Sure," he said. "Let's watch it."

I walked past Jerôme's chair to the back room, wheeled the T.V. out and set it up. When I got it tuned in to the right channel, I looked at Jerôme and said,

"Feature race is on. Can't miss that."

He gave me a questionable look, and I turned and went to my chair and rotated it so Chad could see the race when it started. In the meantime, I kept working on the haircut. If I could finish it up by post time, things'd work out real good. The horses were parading past the camera heading for the post when Chad said,

"Who's go'n'a win it, Bernie?"

"My money's on Kauai King with Blumfield up. I don't see how he can lose, even though he's carrying a hundred and twenty-five pounds."

As I finished dusting off his neck, it was post time, and Bradley Nims came in followed by Asa. Chad no sooner stepped down than Joe Hernández announced,

"There they go."

We were all standing around my chair watching the horses race around the track. Jerôme, Jorge Ballesteros and

133

Joe Cockburn were standing around Jerôme's chair, also watching.

*   *   *

When the race was over (and Kauai King did win it), the shop cleared out except Mister Nims, who sat down in my chair, and Jorge, who got into Jerôme's chair. Jorge, Jerôme's last customer, had come in early. He brought in a six-pack, so he, Jerôme and I had one. Mister Nims wasn't drinking. He took off his wire-rim glasses and gave them to me before he sat down.

"How's Denny doing these days?" I asked.

"Fine, fine," he said. "He just got his scholarship approved for next year. Now all he's got'a do is finish up his last year and pass the bar. Then he can start practicing law."

"I hope he has an easier time figuring out legal language than I do," I said. "If you ever read about a trial in the paper or hear some of the decisions the courts make, you'd think lawyers and judges had a language all their own. It sure don't sound much like English."

"Better get used to it, my friend, 'cause that's how it's go'n'a be from now on. Our society is becoming more technical every day, and this applies to the language in all these different fields. Last week I went shopping with my wife. While she was at the butcher's counter, she sent me over to get olives. She told me she didn't want large olives, so I went looking for some small olives. Problems from the start. There was every kind of olive except large, medium and small. They had jumbo olives, giant olives and miniature olives. I couldn't believe it.

One And Two Halves

"The point is that in today's world, one's language needs to be as precise as possible so that he or she can communicate relevant and important information in the most effective way possible."

About then, Jerôme asked,

"You want another beer, Bernie?"

"Still got a half a bottle, thanks."

"Suit yourself. I'm havin' another one."

Nims must've thought I was asleep because I didn't respond to anything he'd said, and he was looking at me like he expected me to. I really didn't give a damn about his olives. All I wanted was to finish his haircut and get him on his way.

"Yeah, I see what yuh mean," I laughed, as I towel-dried his hair.

A busy day was coming to an end, so it seemed like things were moving faster. It certainly didn't take me the full half hour to finish Mister Nims's haircut. I turned his back to the big mirror on the backbar and held the hand mirror up so he could see the taper.

"It looks fine, just fine," he said smiling behind his wire-rim glasses.

He took his sweater off the coat rack by the front door and got his checkbook out of the sagging pocket. After he got it spread out on the counter next to the register, he took some yellow notepaper out of it and put it next to the checkbook. I gave him a pen, and he wrote a check for five dollars and left the shop.

I took the check over to my backbar, stamped it and took it back to the register. It was when I put it inside that I noticed the folded yellow notepaper next to the register. I picked it up and ran out the door, but it was too late. Mister

135

Nims had disappeared. So, I took it back into the shop and set it down in front of the radio on top of the note that Herb White had left earlier.

*   *   *

When I caught my breath, I walked to the back of the shop and got the broom and gave the place a good clean sweep down. Then I went back to my chair and washed my face. That sure was a pleasure. There was nothing like hot water splashed in your face after a long day of cutting hair.

I went over to the register and started counting the money. I wasn't there a minute before Jerôme came over with five dollars from Jorge. I put it in and took all the tickets off the spindle and separated them. Eight of them were Jerôme's and I had fifteen. Pretty busy day, I thought. I counted the money and it came out right. Forty for Jerôme and seventy-five for me. I took the money and put it in my wallet and went to the back room to get my jacket. After Jorge left, Jerôme went to the restroom. By the time he came out, I'd shut all the lights off, closed the blinds and was sitting in my chair waiting for him. When I turned the radio off, I noticed the yellow notepaper Mister Nims had left behind on top of the letter Herb'd left earlier. I unfolded it and read,

"Dear Jesus,
Bless Beth and Denny and Virginia and please help me with my weight problem. Demon gluttony is causing me to be overweight. Please help me with that. Please help me to be financially independent. I am in your hands. I expect you

136

One And Two Halves

to take over my complete life. I expect you to help me with my business deals. I love you Jesus.

Bradley"

I crumpled it up and threw it in the wastepaper basket.

"You ready to split?" Jerôme said. He had his jacket on and his beer in his hand.

"No hurry," I said. "We can relax and finish our beers."

"We did have a hell of a busy day, didn't we?"

"Sure did. You did eight cuts and I did fifteen."

"Well, I've got'a split," he said, as he tossed his empty into the trash. "I'm go'n'a meet Randall and his wife across the street."

"Was that that swell looking tomato that was in here a couple hours ago talking to the guy in your chair?"

"That's the one. Wasn't she fine?"

"I'll say!"

"I'm outa' here. See yuh in the morning."

"Okay. See yuh then."

It was now my turn to take my place out on the street, so I took one last look at the shop to make sure everything was in its place. Then I locked the door and headed for my car.

The End

1969-2019

Tales of the Iron Chair

For Sam Téllez and Bill Sey

"…COME BACK A SHORT DISTANCE
CORRECTLY"
Edward Albee

Saturday, August 9, 1975

I

I pass the green sign on the side of the road. I'm about ten minutes from the shop. The sign says:
Half Moon Bay
City Limits

Elev. 70   Pop. 5,167

Only three more miles to go. The whole trip was overcast and foggy, and it looks like that's the way it's go'n'a be for the rest of the day here. Lota' days the fog line starts at Pigeon Point. Not today. It was foggy in Santa Cruz when I left home, but I bet it burns off down there by noon. That's the difference between here and there. Last summer, which was my last one living on the Coastside, there was no sun from Memorial Day to Labor Day. At least it comes out in the afternoon in Santa Cruz this time of year. It's an interesting little weather pocket. I can stand on the cliff at Steamer Lane any day of the week and watch the fog line stretch

One And Two Halves

from Pigeon Point to Monterey. That whole peninsula and on south past Morro Bay is usually fogged in. You've got'a go to Pismo Beach before you get back into the sun.

I'm go'n'a have to start thinking about finding someplace to cut hair in Santa Cruz. I've been doing the commute six months now, and it's starting to wear on me. I need to get a job closer to home, so I can get back on my bike more, like how I used to do when I was cutting hair in Belmont Shore and taking classes at Long Beach State. In those days I went everywhere on my bike. For the last six years, since I moved north, I've been getting everywhere in the car, and I'm really getting tired of all the driving. The only saving grace to this commute is the scenery along Highway One, and half of that's go'n'a disappear in another couple month's with the time change. Unless I find something closer to home, my drive back to Santa Cruz will be in the dark. Highway One between Half Moon Bay and Santa Cruz is no place to be after dark. You don't wan'a break down out there, for sure.

It's pretty amazing how suburban sprawl has spread in this area since when I first moved here five years ago. The shopping center I'm passing here at the corner of Highway One and Highway Ninety-two wasn't here five years ago. Some of the houses I'm coming to on the left were in the final stages of construction. They were just finishing the last ones when we moved to El Granada. Dolger Tract, just north of El Granada across the highway from the airport and Princeton, was another recent tract development in the area. It was named after the developer, Henry Dolger, who'd developed all of Westlake after the war. More recent developments, not by Dolger or Dean and Dean, are Sea Haven and Frenchman's Creek, right here on my right. I think this horse ranch's days are numbered over here on the left.

141

Jerome Arthur

As I pass Miramar Beach, I notice that there's a little bit of sun shining up in the El Granada Highlands. It probably won't spread down to the Flats, which is where my shop is. I take my right at the turn-off at the south end of El Granada. I follow Alhambra up to my shop, which is in a small strip center with a view of Pillar Point harbor and the ocean beyond. Also located in the center are a library, which occupies about a third of the space in the building, a contractor, a cable T.V. office on one side of me, and a beauty shop on the other side.

I often ask myself how I ever got to this place in the fog. My best friend in graduate school at Long Beach State got me pointed in this direction. He and his wife stayed in our apartment for the two weeks that my wife and I were gone to Hawaii on our honeymoon. When we got back, we took weekend trips to different towns along the California coast in the hope of finding some place outside the Los Angeles basin to move to. We'd both been raised there, and by the time we got married, we were tired of it. It had grown too much for either of our liking, thus the thought of getting out. Our only criterion was that wherever we moved, it would have to be close to the beach. So, at the end of a three-day weekend, I got a call from my grad. school buddy.

"I think I've found the place you wan'a move to," he said. "Santa Cruz. Up the coast a little way from Monterey."

By that time we'd looked in Ventura, Santa Barbara, Morro Bay, Dana Point (though I never was crazy about Orange County), Fallbrook (which wasn't close enough to the beach for my liking), and Oceanside. We hadn't yet gone north of San Luis Obispo. So, we took a trip to Santa Cruz, and when we got there, I realized that we should've skipped all the rest and started there in the first place. We stopped at Cabrillo College first. I got an application for a position in

142

One And Two Halves

the English department. My wife picked up applications at three elementary school districts in the county. We spent one day and overnight there and fell in love with the place.

We got our applications in and waited to hear. I got no response from Cabrillo, but she got calls for interviews from Scotts Valley and Live Oak. She landed a fourth-grade position at Brook Knoll School in Scotts Valley, and we moved to Aptos.

The best I could do was a haircutting job in Live Oak. By spring I got an evening college job seventy-five miles away at Skyline College in San Bruno. That same semester I landed a tutoring job at Cabrillo. In February we learned that we were pregnant, so my wife finished out her contract at Brook Knoll in June, and we moved to El Granada to be closer to Skyline, where I was hoping to eventually get a full-time tenure-track teaching position. That was five years ago, and that job never materialized, so I got back into cutting hair at a time when hairstyling was taking off.

We'd bought a house in Montara a year before I opened the shop in El Granada. It looked like we'd be settling down in the Half Moon Bay area, when one spring weekend last year, we went down to Santa Cruz to visit friends. We dressed in our warm woolies and turned on the windshield wipers when we got out onto Highway One. By the time we passed Pigeon Point, it was so warm and sunny that we were peeling off our layers, and when we got to the Beacon station on the corner of Mission and Chestnut, we saw a young couple on the sidewalk wearing only cutoffs and go-aheads. The woman was wearing a bikini top.

"Would yuh look at that," I said.

"They're looking pretty comfortable, aren't they?" said Ella.

143

Jerome Arthur

"What the hell're we doin' living up in that God forsaken foggy place. We moved up north to live in *Santa Cruz*. We oughta' think seriously about moving back here."

"Be okay with me. Didn't you say Fred Lane is a customer of yours? Give 'im a call tomorrow and put the house on the market."

And so we did. Like I say, we went all summer without ever seeing the sun. Needless to say, the house didn't sell after a ninety-day listing, so we took it off the market for the holiday season and tried again with more success after the first of the year. By last spring we'd moved back to Santa Cruz, and I've been commuting Highway One ever since.

It's five to ten as I pull into the parking lot of the center where my shop is, and my first client isn't here yet. Herb is behind his desk in the construction office, and Joleen is behind hers in the cable T.V. office. I wave to both as I approach my front door, and they wave back. Camille isn't in the beauty shop yet. As I get the shop ready to start cutting, Ken Hopkins comes in. He's holding what looks like an L. P.

"'Mornin' Ken. How's it goin'?"

"Hey, Jerôme. 'S happenin'?"

*   *   *

The first thing I do after I get inside is turn the lights and radio on. It's a tube radio, so it takes a few extra seconds to warm up. When the sound starts coming out of the speaker, Steely Dan is singing, "Rikki Don't Lose That Number." It's tuned to KSAN. Then I roll up the bamboo shade in the front window. I take a minute to check out my view. The sailboats anchored in Pillar Point Harbor look so peaceful. I

144

can't see if there are any surfers outside the jetty. Fog shrouds the Navy dish at the end of the Point.

Wednesday and Saturday are my two favorite days in the shop. I've got my schedule set up so that I'm only cutting on Tuesday, Wednesday, Friday and Saturday. I get to spend tomorrow, Sunday and Monday in Santa Cruz. I went to the four-day schedule when I started the long commute. That was last March. My book is filled from ten to four on those four days.

As I head to the back to hang up my windbreaker, I see Camille out of the corner of my eye going by my window. She's opening up her beauty shop next door. Ken grabs a *National Geographic* and sits down in my chair. As I come back up front, Joleen goes by and into Camille's shop. Probably making an appointment to get her hair done.

Ken's a good example of someone who's been wearing his hair long from a young age. In '68 when I left Bernie after I got my M.A. degree and went in search of a junior college teaching job, the only people who were wearing long hair were hippies and radical college students. In fact, '68 was the year I started using the four-aught blade to shave my own head. I did it for two reasons: I was trying to get out of the hair business and into teaching, and I was just flat-out being contrary. Ken here, who's a recording engineer in the City, has probably had long hair since he was in high school in the mid-sixties. It's still long and wavy. It's go'n'a take me the full forty-five minutes I've got him scheduled for.

I've been doing what's called "hairstyling" for about ten years now. Bernie and I started doing shampoo cuts after the first hair seminar we attended, but we were doing mostly short hairstyles back then. We never really learned how to work with long hair. I had to take some more classes a cou-

145

ple years ago to get the technique down. Right now, most of the work I do is on heads like Ken's.

"So, how're things at Wally Heider?" I say.

"Great. I actually brought you a record," he says handing over the L.P. I saw him holding when he came in.

"Oh, wow! Thanks a lot," I say, as I look at the album. "*Child of Nature*, Jack Traylor and Steelwind. Yuh know, they play this song a lot on KSAN."

"Yeah, I know. I've actually spoken to Stefan Ponek. He says he's gotten a lot of requests for it after he played it a couple times."

"That's pretty cool," I say.

I ease his head back into the shampoo bowl. As I'm lathering him up, he says,

"I got the coolest job. I get to meet all these cool people, like Carlos Santana who was in the studio last week working on a new album. He's really a nice guy."

"Wow, that sounds so cool."

We don't talk as I shampoo and condition his hair. That's the one thing you got'a do on long hair, condition it to get the tangles out. When I finish, I get him back in an upright position and start working on the cut. His hair is maybe eight inches long, parted in the center. I'm taking off about an inch all over.

"I'll bring you a copy of the Santana album when it gets pressed."

"That'd be cool. How'd you ever get into the recording business?"

"Been interested in it since I was in high school. Ended up taking some classes in recording technology at City College. 'Fact I was at City the same time as O.J. Simpson."

"Really?"

One And Two Halves

"Yeah, but I never heard of him till he got to U.S.C. And then I never really paid too much attention to what he was doing 'cause I've never been interested in football. It's more fun hanging out in the recording studio."

"Yeah, I can see where it would be."

"So, wha'da yuh think about the cropa' Democrats that might be runnin' for president next year?"

"Little too early to tell, but of the ones I've heard about, I kinda' like Fred Harris, myself. Yuh know, the guy from Oklahoma?"

"Yeah, I know 'im. I like 'im too. He's a populist, right?"

"Yeah, that's why I like 'im. He's also got some Cherokee blood I hear."

"I heard that too."

"First time in eight years that Vietnam ain't go'n'a be the main issue."

"Yeah and thank God for that."

I'm working right along here. I've taken off about an inch all around, and now I'm working on the design line around the bottom. As I finish that, I get out my Denman brush and start blowing it dry. When I was working for Bernie, we didn't use the blow dryer much because we were doing butches, flattops and Ivy League hairstyles, and those would dry pretty good with just a towel. The only kind of length then was the rockabilly hairstyle, but it was on the way out. You really need a blow dryer on hair like Ken's. It's long and thick and wavy. But you don't want to over-dry it. You want it to be ever so slightly damp when you're finished.

As I'm hanging the blow dryer back on the hook, Ray, my next cut, comes in. He's about five minutes early, which is fine. Better early than late. I get Ken's face lined up in the hand mirror which gives him a clear shot at the back of his head. I'm looking at it myself, and it looks sharp. Hair a woman would kill for.

"How's 'at, Ken?"

"Good."

"Okay, we're done. Good for another thousand miles, huh?"

"No doubt. How much I owe yuh?"

"Ten bucks."

He takes fifteen out of his wallet, hands it over, and asks for two bucks change. I give him his change and schedule his next haircut. He heads out the door and says,

"See yuh next month, Jerôme."

"All right, see yuh later, Ken."

*   *   *

He leaves and Ray gets in the chair.

When I first started cutting Ray's hair in Stan's shop up in Pacifica, he told me to call him Ray, but it should be Lou. It's Louis Raymond rather than the other way around. Ray's a good example of how the longer hairstyles have hit the middle class. He's maybe ten years older than I, so he's from a generation that grew up wearing crewcuts. Elvis Presley's hairstyle was even too radical for him, no doubt. So now here he is forty-five years old in the mid-seventies with his salt and pepper hair growing down over his ears and a little over his collar.

He still uses a lacquer spray to hold it in place. I've tried to sell him some of my Redken ph balanced spray, but he says it doesn't hold as well as the Aquanet he buys at the

One And Two Halves

Thrifty Drug Store in the shopping center in Half Moon Bay. He *is* using the Redken Jellasheen shampoo I sell him.

"How yuh want yer hair cut today, Ray?"

"Keep it down over the ears and block it in back at the collar. Take about a half inch off the top."

"You got it," I say, dropping the chair back so his head goes into the sink.

"Looks like the Niners're go'n'a have a good fuckin' team this year," Ray says. "They got rid a' that fuckin' Spurrier and brought in Snead from the Giants."

"Ain't he gettin' a little old?"

"Yeah, he is. Prob'ly the end of his fuckin' career."

He's talking outa' the side of his mouth in a low voice, like he wants to keep everything on the Q.T., and no one else in the shop except him and me. He stops talking once I start shampooing his hair.

"Think the Niners'll make it to the Super Bowl this year?" I say, already knowing the answer.

They won't even come close to winning their division. One of the reasons I haven't gotten into following the Forty-Niners since I moved north is because they have such a lousy team. They're never even go'n'a go to the Super Bowl much less win it. I'm still a Rams fan.

"I doubt it," he says. "Got'a win their fuckin' division first. Then they got'a win the conference, and that's go'n'a be tough for them for what they got."

Ray's a real sports fan. It's all he ever talks about when I'm cutting his hair. In spring and summer, it's all Giants baseball; in fall and winter, it's Forty-Niners football; in winter and spring, it's Warriors basketball. There is no hockey team in the Bay Area, and if there were, I'm sure Ray'd be talking about them. It's ironic that he roots for the Giants when the A's in Oakland got a better team. Since I'm not

149

that big of a sports fan anymore, I don't know what else to say to him. He seems to be out of things to talk about, so I just keep cutting his hair. I'm finished with the finger work on top, so I pull the long side hair down and cut a blunt line along the top of the earlobe at the canal.

"Hey, Jerôme, reach over and get me that *Sports Il-lustrated*."

I go over to the wooden cable reel I use for a table, pick up the magazine, step back to the chair and give it to him. When I finish cutting his hair, I towel dry the little moisture left in it from the shampoo. Before I turn the blower on, he says out of the side of his mouth on the Q.T., holding the magazine up like he's pretending to look at it,

"So, yuh ever go'n'a get someone to work that second chair?"

"Probably not. I been working these last three years alone, and I kinda' like it. Not that it wasn't fun working with Stan. He's a cool guy and a lot of fun to be around, but I'm liking it like this."

I haven't told him that I won't be here that much longer. He knows I moved to Santa Cruz, but I haven't told him I'm lookin' to get outa' the commute.

"I quit getting' into Stan's fuckin' chair 'cause of all the action he had goin' in the back room. I was afraid he was go'n'a get busted while he was cuttin' my hair."

He had a point there. Stan used to have illegal fire-works around Fourth of July and Super 8 pornographic films all year 'round, all in the back room.

"Yeah," I say. "I used to worry about that, too. He didn't believe me, though, when I told him he was scaring away business. I tried to tell 'im, but I couldn't get through to 'im."

One And Two Halves

"Fuckin' guy didn't see he's scaring business away?"

"Guess not. He still hasn't quit doin' it. Guess I'm pretty lucky you didn't go to another shop."

"Hey, I's getting' ready to, but you moved down here, and that worked out great, 'cause it's closer to home."

"Yeah, this is only down the hill for you, and you don't have to go over Devil's Slide just to get a haircut."

The phone rings and when I pick it up, I hear Jim Rice's voice on the other end.

"Hey, Jerôme. What's goin' on? Yuh got any time for me on Tuesday morning?"

I look at my book and can see I've only got one opening on Tuesday.

"How's ten-forty-five Tuesday mornin' sound?"

"Good, put me down."

I'm doing the finishing touches on Ray's hair. When I'm done, I pick up the hand mirror and walk around in front of him and line him up so he can see the back of his head.

"How's 'at look, Ray?"

"Pretty fuckin' good."

"Okay," I say. "That's it."

As I'm putting the mirror away, I look out the front window and see Carl Dobbs parking his car across the parking lot by the street. I take the towel and dust the loose hairs off of his nape. Then I take the vacuum and pick up what's left. As I take off the haircloth, he gets out of the chair and walks over to the cash box Haney made for me in his wood shop class at Pescadero High. I follow him and wait with the lid open for him to get some money out of his wallet. Then he reaches down to the products rack and picks up an eight-ounce bottle of Jellasheen.

"Is this stuff any fuckin' good?" he asks.

151

"Yeah. You use it. Don't yuh like it?"

"It's okay. How much I owe yuh?"

"Ten for the cut, two for the bottle a' shampoo."

He gives me a twenty-dollar bill and tells me to give him seven bucks change.

"Thanks, Ray. See you in a month, okay?"

"Yeah kid," he says out of the side of his mouth. "See you then."

He passes Dobbs on his way out.

*   *   *

Carl gets in my chair, and I go back to work. It's coming up on eleven-thirty and I'm right on schedule. Dobbs is a very cool cat, one of my favorite clients. He's a big-time golf fan, and amateur golfer with a twelve handicap. He follows the P.G.A. tour religiously and thinks Arnold Palmer is the greatest player ever. He considers Jack Nicklaus an upstart and refers disparagingly to him as "Chubby." He talks a lot about his own golf game, and how the city league softball team he plays on in Pacifica is doing, but only if they're doing good. He's a real good-time-Charlie, and he's got this good-natured giggle that you can't help but like.

"How's it goin'?" I say, as he sits in the chair.

Carl's got one of those perfect heads of hair where everything falls in place. Like Ray, he's let it grow down over his ears and collar. I wasn't cutting his hair ten years ago, but I bet he was wearing a crewcut. In fact, I know he was because he's told me he wore it that way back then.

"Okay," he says. "How about yourself?"

"I'm okay. Except for the damn commute. Tired before I even cut a head."

One And Two Halves

"Now you know what it's been like for me for the last ten years."

"Yeah, but you're commute's only about twenty miles. Mine's fifty. Big difference."

"Hey, your commute's Highway One from Santa Cruz to El Granada. Mine's over Devil Slide, through Pacifica and Daly City. Big difference."

He's got a point there. Mine's longer, but more beautiful and peaceful, no traffic. He's got a short but hectic drive in heavy traffic by comparison. And then he's not done driving after he gets to the City. He's a dental supply salesman, so he's on the road traveling all over the Bay Area every day.

"Looks like Chubby's go'n'a win this year's P.G.A.," he says, and giggles that infectious giggle of his.

"No kiddin'. That's goin' on right now?"

I'm not much of a sports fan, especially golf.

"They'll be wrapping it up tomorrow, and it looks like Nicklaus's got it in the bag."

"How's your boy, Palmer, go'n'a do?"

"Not in it. He's doin' the Ryder Cup Matches this year. Captain of the team."

"What's that?"

"Team play."

"Hm. Never heard of it."

"You do know he designed the course down here south of town, don't you?"

"Yeah, I heard that. Pretty cool course, too, huh?"

"Very cool. Lot like Pebble Beach."

The phone rings and I pick it up. It's Trevor's mom. She wants to get him in for his back-to-school haircut. Seems kind of early since school doesn't start for another month. I gave Jim my last opening on Tuesday, but I still

153

have a few left on Wednesday, so I offer her my first one at ten o'clock. I go straight back to Carl's haircut. I'm getting close to finishing up.

"Saw Bang last week," he says as I turn on the blow dryer.

Bang is Doctor Banghardt, a dentist whose hair I used to cut in Stan's shop in Pacifica. I was blown away when I found out he was at Los Alamitos when I was stationed there. He never worked on my teeth, but one of my good Navy buddies was a patient of his. I don't know how he ever got located up here. Last I heard he had a practice in Belmont Heights. That was ten years ago. Anyway, Carl and Bang are golfing buddies.

Whether on the golf course or on the job, Carl's a sharp dresser. One time back in the day when I was cutting till six p.m., he came in around five on his way home from work, and I got to see him in the threads he wears when he's on the job. He had on a really expensive-looking three-piece gabardine suit, so it's only natural for him to get his hair styled to match the image. Even when he's dressed casual, like today, he's spotless. I can just picture him on the golf course—orange or lime green sport shirt, checkered trousers, and brown and white saddle shoes with golf spikes.

"Haven't cut his hair in more'n three years," I say. "Since I opened up down here."

As I hang the dryer up, he says, "Yuh know, Jerôme, if you didn't live so far away, you could try out for the slow pitch team I play on."

"Should'a' asked me couple a' years ago when I was still living in Montara. I think it would 'a' been cool to play on your team. I was in better shape back then, too."

I look out the window and see Dave Meredith parking his car next to Carl's. Then I take the haircloth off, and

One And Two Halves

Carl gets out of the chair. I take the lid off the cash box, and he gives me twelve dollars and leaves.

*   *   *

Dave has come in and is sitting in the waiting chair closest to the window. When I get back to my chair, he comes over and sits down. My last cut of the morning. I'm hungry, ready for a break.

"How's it goin', Dave?"

"Not bad. You?"

"Great."

It's about 11:45 when I get going on Dave's haircut. He's been coming in ever since I opened up here three years ago. He's the manager of the Shorebird, the new restaurant over in Princeton across the highway at Pillar Point Harbor. That's one of the first projects that Dean and Dean did on the Coastside. Dave's buddies with one of the partners. Dean and Dean is an Orange County developer brought in by Westinghouse, the corporation that owns most of the land around here. It's the same outfit that developed the golf course. Most of the environmentalists in the area think they want to make the Coastside into Orange County north. It'll never happen. The Orange County coast is sunny year-round. This is more like some places in the British Isles.

Dave's got wavy strawberry blond hair that's down over his ears and collar. He looks like a Southern California surfer who cleaned up his act. He dresses casually, but clean-cut, khaki chinos and short sleeve sport shirt, not unlike Carl. He's told me some surfing stories about when he was hanging out with Hobie Alter and Jack Haley surfing the breaks along the southern Orange and northern San Diego county

155

coasts. Spots like San Clemente, San Onofre and Trestles down at Camp Pendleton.

The Shorebird, like all the Dean and Dean projects, including the golf course south of town, and Frenchman's Creek north of it, is about the classiest joint in the harbor area. That company really is trying to do some upscale development around here, maybe a little *too* upscale for the Coastside. These little towns along this highway from Mira Mar Beach to El Granada, Moss Beach, and Montara up near Devil's Slide only have one paved street for cars to drive on. All the other streets are dirt or gravel with on sidewalks.

Back to Dave here. He's got the same kind of class as the restaurant he works in. He knows a lot of high rollers, and he knows a lot about them. Plus, he keeps what he knows to himself. Which is fine with me. He's still surfing, so that's what we talk about. He surfs the ankle snappers right out in front here across the highway, outside the jetty. He also drives down to Santa Cruz and catches waves down there.

"So, you been out lately?" I ask.

"Did dawn patrol the other day at low tide. Was *nice*. About knee- to waist-high. Very cool."

"You ever go out to Maverick's?"

"You kidding? Those waves're too big for me. Does anybody surf out there?"

"I got this customer who's a junior at Half Moon Bay High, and he says he's got a buddy who just started surfing that break last winter. My client says his buddy's the only guy out there. My guy says he just sits up on the cliff and watches. Won't go out there himself. Damn waves're twenty-five feet high."

"Yeah, I've gone out to the cliff and looked. Too big for me."

156

One And Two Halves

"How's the surf up here compare to Southern California surf?"

"Lot better up here. More point breaks; down there it's mostly beach breaks. Santa Cruz is better than the Coastside. They got a lota' good spots. One of my favorites is Four Mile."

"Yeah, I heard about it. When I's living in Nastrini Arms over by Corky's, one of my neighbors used to surf that break."

Nastrini Arms is a flat-roof five-plex a couple blocks from here. That's not the official name. I just called it that because the place was so run-down, with a leaky roof and paper-thin walls, that I thought giving it a classy name might improve it. Nastrini's the name of the absentee landlady who owns the place. She lives over the hill in San Mateo.

"Besides being a good break," Dave says, "you don't have to go all the way into Santa Cruz to surf there."

"Looks like it gets crowded. I always see a buncha' cars parked there when I drive by on my way up here."

"That definitely happens, but it's not consistently as crowded as Steamer Lane, down by that lighthouse in town."

By now, I'm towel drying Dave's hair. He likes to keep it looking curly so I don't use the blow dryer. That just makes curly hair look frizzy.

"We should schedule my next haircut earlier in the day. This is probably the busiest time for me in the restaurant. Ten o'clock would be better."

"No problem. Just tell me when you call. So, you know what's the next big project for Dean and Dean?"

"I think they're puttin' together a master plan for the corner of Ninety-two and One. Eventually there's go'n'a be shopping centers on all those corners."

157

"Boy, how're the environmentalists go'n'a like that?"

"Probably not very much. They're moving through the planning process, and you can bet the environmentalists're go'n'a show up at all the hearings to protest it."

"No doubt."

"Prob'ly the biggest roadblock's go'n'a be this new Coastal Commission. They're go'n'a be tough when they first start out. But Dean and Dean'll make out okay because of the quality of their projects. They're not go'n'a build anything like this little tract north of town here, yuh know, across the highway from the airport."

"Dolger Tract. I had a guy in my chair once who was a contractor on the second stage of that development. Yuh know the ones out in front? He told me they were two-by-two construction shot with some kinda' foam."

"Hey, I believe it. Dean and Dean won't be doing anything like that. Strictly upscale stuff."

The clock on the wall says it's about ten after noon. I'm doing the finishing touches on Dave's haircut. I show him the haircut in the hand mirror, and he says,

"Looks good."

"Okay, that's it then," I say and take the haircloth off.

We walk together around to right behind the second chair where I have a desk I've had since my teaching days. I lift the lid off the cash box. He hands me fifteen bucks and asks for three back. I give him the change and he turns and leaves.

*　　　*　　　*

One And Two Halves

So that's it for the morning. It's afternoon and the fog's still thick. I clean up my tools, put them away, and sweep around my chair. Then I lock up and go over to El Granada Market. I go straight back to the butcher's counter and order up some ham and Swiss cheese slices from Brogan. Then I go over to the cold box and pick up a bottle of cream soda. On my way back to the shop, I wave to the two surfers who live in number five at Nastrini Arms. They pass me in their pickup truck; their boards and wetsuits are stashed in the bed.

Back in the shop, I spread my lunch out on the desk, turn the volume up on the radio and listen to Van Morrison singing "Madame George."

*   *   *

My next customer is Roland Dark. I used to cut his hair when I was working for Bernie in Belmont Shore. He's coming in with his best buddy, Chuck McBain, who was also a customer of mine in Long Beach. These guys work for Shell Oil Company and they did then, too. They go way back. They roomed together all through college and have been working for the same company since they graduated. The last time I saw either of them before they started coming here was 1966. Chuck had just gotten transferred up to Shell's Northern California headquarters in San Francisco. At the time Roland was expecting a similar transfer, and indeed it came shortly after Chuck's. They both live out in Walnut Creek and commute to the City on Bart. Since they moved up here, they've made it a habit to come to the Coastside once a month, or so, for lunch. One weekend last year when they were here, they were cruising through El Granada, and when they saw the shop, they decided to get

159

haircuts. I was really surprised when they came through my door. They've been regulars once a month ever since. Their wives drop them off in the parking lot and they go over to the antique shop in Princeton.

"So, who's first?" I say.

They look at each other, and then Roland steps forward. I put the haircloth on him and drop him back into the sink. He wears his thin, slightly wavy hair too long. I say "too long" because it's so thin. He's even got a bald spot in the crown area. It'll only grow so long when it's that thin, and then the ends start breaking and the hair starts looking stringy. Roland never has let his hair get too long, even in Long Beach nine years ago. He and Chuck both like to keep it trimmed.

Chuck is sitting in the chair next to the front window and is reading a *New Yorker*.

"So, you guys still liking your jobs up here?" I say. "Still moving up the ladder?"

"We're getting there. Chuck's closer'n me. He's one step ahead of me."

"Yuh know, last time you were in we didn't talk too much about those other guys you used to hang with in the Shore. Ever hear anything from Gary Kelly or Joe Cockburn? Those were two cool guys."

"I'm in touch with both of 'em. Have been since I moved north. I told 'em how you're cutting our hair again. Gary actually got his law degree and got a job with a small firm. Doin' estate planning."

"Wow! Pretty cool."

"Cockburn moved over to Standard and he's moving up that ladder there. Number one expert in logging. Really knows his geology."

One And Two Halves

Throughout this conversation, Chuck's been engrossed in something in *The New Yorker.* He hasn't heard a word we've said. He looks up from the magazine and says,

"Can I borrow this magazine, bring it back next time I come in? I don't think I can finish this article before we leave."

"Hey, take it with you and keep it. One of my other customers brings 'em in, and I'm always ending up with a stack of 'em." Then I turn back to Roland and say, "So, how do yuh like livin' so far away from the beach? Didn't you guys used to live in the Shore when you were down south?"

"Yeah, we did, and when we were in Washington, too. That's why we come down here once a month, but Walnut Creek's really nice. Lots of sunshine."

"You have way better weather than over here. 'S why I moved back to Santa Cruz. Best beach weather north of Santa Barbara. Don't think I could've lasted here through another summer."

"Yeah, well you're up here every day anyway."

"Not every day. Four days. That gives me three days of sunshine. Some days we get morning fog, but it burns off by noon most times, a lot like Long Beach. Up here it doesn't burn off all summer. The way it was last year, my last summer in this godforsaken place."

"Hope you don't move your operation down there anytime soon. Lot farther away from Walnut Creek than here. 'Sides we just found you again."

"Haven't found any place to cut hair down there that suits me, but I'm lookin'. Don't worry, I'll give yuh plenty a' notice. 'Least a month."

"Did I tell you we're goin' to the Niners' first exhibition game next month?"

161

"No. Where is that go'n'a be, and who're they playing?"

"Out at the Stick. They're playing the Raiders."

"It's become a tradition with us. This'll be the third year we've done it. A whole group of us from the office do a tailgate scene in the parking lot. It's pretty cool."

"'Sounds like fun. You guys go to any season games?"

"Yeah, couple. Don't have season tickets or anything like that, but we do go to a couple games. Same thing with the tailgate party."

"Wow! C'n you believe it? It's been a year since Nixon resigned. I's watchin' the news last night and old Cronkite had a story on it. Yesterday was the first anniversary. Man, am I ever glad he's gone? Bad guy!"

"Yeah, I voted for 'im twice. What a mistake."

"No shit. I never voted for that prick. My first vote ever was in sixty-two, and I voted for Pat Brown against Nixon for California governor. I voted for McCarthy in '68 and McGovern last time. 'Fact that vote in seventy-two was the best one I ever cast for president. Worst was my first— Goldwater in sixty-four, but I'd do it again. That's how much I disliked Johnson. He blew it in Vietnam, but I do have to admit, he was right on with the civil rights stuff he got passed and Medicare. Goldwater would've never done any of that."

"My first was in sixty-four, Johnson," Roland says with a grimace.

This is one of my easier cuts today. I'm already doing the finishing touches, cleaning up around his ears and the back of his neck. When I'm satisfied with the haircut and show it to him in the mirror, he says,

"Looks fine."

162

One And Two Halves

I dust off his neck and take the haircloth off.

After he pays me, he sits down in a waiting chair, and Chuck steps up.

"Bring that magazine over here," I say to Chuck, gesturing to the countertop that separates the shampoo bowls. "That way you won't forget it."

*　　　*　　　*

Chuck sits in the chair and I drape the haircloth over him. I used to cut five or six guys from Shell Oil Company when I worked for Bernie, and I always thought then and still do that Chuck was probably the smartest one of them all. He and Joe Cockburn. Before he answers a question or starts talking, he takes time to think about it, and then when he does speak, he always says something smart. It's like if he can't say something intelligent, he won't say anything at all. He used to wear his hair ivy-league style, very conservative, very much the junior executive of that time. Now the junior executive look is long over the ears (covering all or at least half of the ear), and long over the collar.

"So, how'd you make out on that house you bought before you left Huntington Beach?" I ask as I'm lathering up his hair.

He'd put money down on a brand-new house before he left Southern California. He hadn't even moved in when he got the transfer. Hell, the place wasn't even finished.

"You remember that? You've got a good memory. It was no problem getting out of that deal. The developer just let us out of it."

"That easy, huh?"

"Yeah. There was a long waiting list to get those homes. He didn't have any trouble selling mine."

163

"Cool."

I move the chair up into the upright position and towel out the excess water. Then I brush out the tangles and start cutting. Chuck's hair's a lot like Mike's, thick and wavy, but not as long.

"Wha'cha reading in *The New Yorker*?"

"An article about Francis Ford Coppola, you know, the director of *The Godfather*?"

"Yeah, I hear it's a cool movie. Brando's supposed to be pretty good in it."

"You haven't seen it?"

"Not yet. Haven't lived near any movie theaters the last five years. Bunch of 'em downtown Santa Cruz. We're go'n'a be goin' to a lot more movies now that we live there."

"Yuh ever get a chance to see this one, go. It's a classic. Writer in *The New Yorker* says it's go'n'a be one of the all-time great movies. Right up there with *Casablanca* and *Citizen Kane*."

"Probably have to catch it at the Nickelodeon. That's a little art theater downtown that shows a lot of foreign films and first run Hollywood pictures on the second go-around. Sash Mill Cinema's another one. They mostly show old movies."

"*Godfather* ever comes back around, you got'a see it."

The conversation stops there for a few minutes, and the shop settles into a silence broken by strains of "Mountain Jam" from the *Eat a Peach* album by the Allman Brothers Band.

"So, Roland says you're go'n'a be tailgating at a Niners' game."

"Yeah. It's go'n'a be fun. I don't really go for the game. It's a big social event for me."

One And Two Halves

"Early pre-season game?"

"Yep."

"You're going at the best time. Later in the season it's too cold and wet at the Stick."

"Hey, you don't know cold and wet till you've been to Seattle."

"That's right, you guys are from up that way, huh? Ain't never been that far up. Been to Portland and Vancouver, Washington, but no farther. So, how's that for an old ex-English teacher, 'ain't never been'?"

"I don't blame you for using whatever kind of language you want to. It's your shop. From the sound of it, your teaching experience wasn't all that great anyway, right?"

"You can say that again. Actually, the classroom experience was pretty good; I just couldn't get on full-time. For three years I was driving up to Skyline College four nights a week. I finally saw the handwriting on the wall; no way was I ever go'n'a get full-time work there."

"Kind of tough to put in all that time and effort and not get anything in return."

"Don't know why I ever went that way in the first place. Such a good gig I've got here. 'Member what I used to say when I was cutting your hair before? 'This isn't like work; this is like hanging out with my best friends for thirty to forty minutes, and when they leave, they give me money.' What more could I ask for?"

"You've got it made."

"Indeed I do. But soon enough, I'm go'n'a be startin' all over again. Don't think I c'n do another winter up here. So, tell me again. When yuh goin' to this game?"

"Early next month."

"Yeah, I'm not so sure the weather's go'n'a be any better then than it is now. You c'n see it ain't go'n'a burn off today, and this weather's not unlike the weather at Candlestick. Indian Summer don't really start till mid-September."

I'm putting the finishing touches on his haircut. I've got him facing the mirror, and I see movement in the parking lot out of the corner of my eye. The guys's wives have pulled the car in and are getting out. I dust off the loose hairs from the back of Chuck's neck, and when I finish, I hold the hand mirror up so he can see the back and profile of his haircut. After getting his approval, I take the haircloth off and he steps out of the chair. We both walk together to the cash box. The wives have come in and are standing next to the front door. Also approaching is my next cut, Megan O'Connor.

*   *   *

Megan's married to another one of my clients. His name is Declan and he's from Ireland. They're moving to Minneapolis, Minnesota, her hometown. They'll be trading the fog for snow. He had a short career with McDonalds. He went to Hamburger University in Chicago, and then became assistant manager for a couple years at the McDonalds in Pacifica. When he got passed over for manager, he decided to quit and look for another career, and that's another reason they're heading to Minnesota. My daughter and their son were classmates in the Co-op Nursery School down in Grandview Terrace. Megan and my wife met there, and that's how Declan started coming to me for haircuts. A year ago I traded her two haircuts for the macramé hanger that my spider plant hangs in, and she's been coming in ever since.

She's got thick dark hair, blunt cut around the bottom, bobbed at the collar. She's a really nice lady, who doesn't necessarily look special when she comes in, but looks great when she leaves. I love my work, and it never

166

gets boring because of the conversation. In fact, I don't even think about the cutting part of it anymore; my hands seem to do it automatically.

"Getting any action on your house?" I say.

Their place is in Dolger Tract. They got one of the newer ones out in front.

"An offer came in on Wednesday, and it'll probably go into escrow on Monday."

"'Soon as it closes, you guys'll be on your way. Think you c'n live in that weather again?"

"It won't be pretty, but I think it'll be okay."

"That's where I was born, yuh know?"

"No, really?"

"Yup. Born in my grandma's living room. 3318 Russell Avenue North. Parents moved to Los Angeles when I was two. Actually, Long Beach. My dad got a job at the Naval Shipyard at Terminal Island in '43. Middle a' the war. And, man, am I lucky they did that. If I'd ha' grown up in Minneapolis, I wouldn't even be alive today. Would've froze to death long time ago."

"I know. I'm not looking forward to the winters."

"One a' the main reasons I moved to Santa Cruz. Warmer and sunnier'n there than here."

"The main reason we're moving to Minnesota is because my dad says he'll hire Declan to be a regional sales manager for his company. Kids'll have grandparents, aunts, uncles and cousins close by. It'll be a welcome change for them. They don't have any of that out here."

"That *is* nice. My in-laws've just moved to Gilroy. It's cool for our daughter."

The afternoon is moving along. Only two more cuts to go. The fog has only lifted slightly. It's still quite gray out there. I can see the Navy dish out on the point. Couple hours ago I couldn't. As I'm looking out the window, Joleen passes by and waves. Probably going to see Camille.

"Boy, I don't know about you, but I'm sure glad I'm getting outa' here," I say. "It's getting way over-developed with the wrong kind of development. Only housing tracts and strip malls anymore. No downtown. Oh, there's Main Street down in Half Moon Bay, but that's three miles away, six from Montara, where I lived before I moved to Santa Cruz. Yuh got'a get on the highway to get from one to the other. You seen the traffic out there lately? Take your life in your own hands if you try to bike it. Lot different in Santa Cruz. They've got this coolest bike path along West Cliff Drive. They're just now finishing up on black topping it. I'm goin' for a bike ride on it tomorrow. I got a route worked out where I only got'a cross one busy street to get to the bike path, and then I take it all the way around the point and end up downtown, where things are happening. Hang out in front a' the Cooper House. Listen to some jazz. It's cool. I feel like I died and went to heaven. They got music there every day. 'Least the days I've been there.''

"It'll be nice living in Minneapolis for that reason, too. City atmosphere."

"I hear Minneapolis is really big in the arts and theater. Had a roommate in Long Beach whose brother was an actor. Those guys were both from Texas, and the brother moved to Minneapolis just because of the opportunities in theater. There's actually quite a bit of that in Santa Cruz, too. For one they have the Barn Theater on the U.C. campus where we saw O'Casey's *The Hostage* last month."

I get talking like this, I tend to quit cutting and just talk, and then I get behind schedule. Fortunately, I give Megan forty-five minutes because of the length and thickness of her hair, so I'm still pretty much on schedule. As I get back

168

One And Two Halves

to working on her hair, I notice my next cut, Lou Minetti, pulling up to the curb in front of the shop in his cherry '64½ Mustang. It isn't a parking place, but Lou's got M.S., and that's about as far as he's able to walk, so I just let him park there. I'm halfway through blowing Megan's hair dry. As slow as Lou is getting around, I should be finished with her by the time he gets in here. I finish the blow dry, unsnap the haircloth, and turn her to face the mirror.

"How's that look, Megan?"

"Good."

"Le'me show you the back."

I turn the chair back around and hold the hand mirror up for her.

"Looks good," she says.

I take the haircloth off, and she steps out of the chair. Before settling with her, I go hold the door open for Lou, who's slowly shuffling in. After he gets in, I go to the cash box and collect ten bucks from Megan.

"Thanks," I say. "Hope your house sells."

"I'm sure it will," she says and leaves.

*　　　*　　　*

As I take Megan's money, Lou shuffles on his cane from the front door to the barber chair. She passes him on her way out.

"How yuh doin', Lou?" I say, as I pick up the haircloth and dust off the chair. "Sit right down."

"Guess I'm doin' good as can be expected. Ailment I got's gettin' worse and worse."

"That's rough. How long you had it?"

"Started to notice symptoms 'bout five years ago. I's only forty-two at the time."

169

"Good thing yuh got yer car. Gives yuh mobility."

"Yeah, and that's a good little car, too. I bought it new January '64 when they first came out."

"It's a cool car."

I'm lathering up his hair, trying to be quick about it. I know this reclined position can't be comfortable for him.

"Wha'da yuh think about the Supreme Court overturning the death penalty?" he asked out of the blue.

"I personally think it's a good deal. I'm totally anti-death penalty."

"I don't know. Maybe it's not such a good idea. How come you're against it?"

"Three good reasons to be against it. Number one—there's always a chance you'll execute the wrong guy. Number two—if the guy's really guilty, it's too easy for him. I say chain 'im to the floor of a cage, and only open it long enough to throw some food in. Number three—it's more expensive, with the appeals and all, to kill the son of a bitch than it is to house and feed 'im for the rest of his life."

"You've got some good points there. I was just thinking if some son of a bitch killed my wife or any of my kids, I'd wan'a see 'im fry."

"I got three words to explain my opposition to the death penalty—'Ruben "Hurricane" Carter.' Know who that is?"

"The fighter?"

"That's right. Black guy. Welter weight. Coulda' been champ. I was a fan of his when he was on top. Sorry son of a bitch was sittin' on death row for almost ten years. Now he's got life without parole. Poor bastard. There's a good chance he didn't commit those murders. There were, I don't know, maybe three, four people shot in a bar in Paterson, New Jersey. Summer a' '66, I think. Two white guys,

170

One And Two Halves

Bellow and Bradley, couple a' small-time crooks were caught red-handed with their fingers in the till surrounded by a buncha' dead bodies. They were the state's main witnesses. Supposed to be eyewitnesses, but they were only trying to get out from under the robbery beef. Probably didn't do it either, but they damn sure didn't see who *did* do it. They said they went into the bar after it happened and were just robbin' the register. Said they saw the getaway car. With some coaxing from the cops, those two bums identified Ruben as the one who did it. Jury was a buncha' gray-haired old white guys. No way Ruben could beat that rap."

The whole time I been talking, I haven't been cutting, so I've gotten a little behind schedule, but at this late hour, it doesn't really matter much. I only got one more cut left.

"I think Ruben's innocent. 'Course I have a long-standing mistrust of the cops. I think they framed 'im."

"Cops've been known to do stuff like that. I think that's what they did to that guy Shepherd in Ohio back in the fifties. Got him convicted of murdering his wife. All circumstantial."

"Exactly what happened to Ruben Carter. Anyway, that's why I'm against the death penalty."

My last cut of the day has just walked in the door and is reading this week's *Time* magazine in the chair by the front window. I dust off the back of Lou's neck and take the haircloth off. He stays seated, reaches for his wallet in the hip pocket of his jeans and hands me twelve bucks.

"Thanks, Lou. See yuh next month."

I take the money back to the cash box as Lou struggles his way out of my chair and starts shuffling toward the front door.

171

Jerome Arthur

*   *   *

Next up, and last of the day, is Charles Jones, a gay man who works in the financial district in San Francisco. He lives alone in a cottage on the way up to El Granada Highlands. Cool guy. Over the years, my gay clients have always been my best clients. I hate to be stereotyping, but it's true, and I don't think it's a bad stereotype. They love what I do for them. They're always complimenting my work. Charles here is like Jorge Ballesteros in that respect. Jorge was another one of my gay customers when I worked with Bernie in the Shore. Charles is just like he was, never has anything bad to say about the cut, only good. He's still got a short haircut in this time of long hair on men. Not a very big guy, kind of petite (another stereotype), but not wiry like a little tough guy, more fragile and swishy.

"So, I think I'm go'n'a get a place up in the City," he says after he's settled in the chair.

"Really? Go'n'a sell your place up the hill?"

"Oh, no. I'll just use it on the weekends. Be my beach house. I'll rent an apartment somewhere around the Castro Street neighborhood."

"How come you're movin' up there?"

"Wan'a work in Harvey Milk's campaign for supervisor. You know about him?"

"Not really. What's his story?"

"He's gay. If he gets elected, he'll be the only openly gay elected official in California. Probably in the country."

"That'll be cool, huh? I'm just glad to hear you're keeping your place down here. Hate to see yuh get your haircut somewhere else."

172

One And Two Halves

I'm not exactly sure why I even said that. It probably won't be long before I'm outa' here for good, myself.

"You don't have to worry about that. I'm coming home weekends. I'll keep my standing appointment, second Saturday of the month."

"So, does this guy have issues other than gay rights, or is that it for him?"

"In fact, that's only a small part of his platform. The one big thing he's done so far is he's gotten this board to pass an ordinance for people to get cited and fined for not cleaning up after their dogs. If he gets elected, he's not go'n'a just represent the gay community; he's go'n'a represent everybody. It's all at-large, no districts."

"What're his chances?"

"Pretty good, but if he doesn't get it this time around, he's go'n'a try again in seventy-seven. He's new to politics."

By now I'm finishing up on topping his hair. Next, I take the towel and get him as dry around the sides and back as I can. Then I take the seven-inch shears and start blending the top with the upper sides and where the taper meets the long hair in back.

"Who yuh likin' for president next year?" I ask as I turn on the clippers.

"I haven't even thought about that one. Too busy working for Harvey. You have a preference?"

"Of all the ones the news people are talking about, I kinda' like Fred Harris, Senator from Oklahoma."

"Call him a populist, right?"

"Right. He claims Cherokee heritage. Figures, being from Oklahoma and all. God, I just hope the Democrats come up with somebody who can win. I'm tired a' these damn Republicans. Corrupt sons a' bitches. I think Nixon ruined it for 'em for a long time."

"Really poisoned the water, didn't he?"

"Well, yeah!"

"You read that book about it, *All the Presidents Men*?"

"Uh, uh. Hear there's go'n'a be a movie coming out later this year. Robert Redford, Dustin Hoffman."

"I haven't read the book. And prob'ly won't, either. Can't wait for the movie. I'll definitely go see it."

I finish the clipper work on the taper and dust off the back of his neck. Then I turn him to face the mirror.

"How's that look," I say.

"Great."

"Good luck on your political campaign. Hope yer guy wins."

"Thanks," he says as he steps out of the chair.

We walk together to the cash box. He gives me fifteen bucks and tells me to keep it. And that's it. I'm done for the day. He leaves and I go to work cleaning up the shop.

*　　　*　　　*

I lock the deadbolt on the front door and head across the parking lot to my Datsun 510 Sedan. So far the car's been doing a good job for my commute, knock on wood. It only takes me a couple minutes to get to the highway, but then, because it's Saturday, that's where things slow down a bit. It's still overcast, but that doesn't seem to have stopped anybody from coming over the hill to hang at the beach. It's not very cold, so maybe that's the attraction. The highway's really go'n'a get crowded in an hour or so when they all start packing up to go home.

174

One And Two Halves

As I drive through Half Moon Bay, I look over at the big stretch of open space on my right where Highway Ninety-two ends. It's wide open all the way down to the surf. Not for long. When I hit the passing lane south of town, I skip around two cars that don't look like they're in as much of a hurry as I am. Traffic has thinned out and I'm humming along. Everything is fine through Tunitas Creek, but when I'm coming down the hill to San Gregorio, my engine starts cutting out on me. It feels like fuel pump or carburetor. As I approach Highway Eighty-four, it starts running smooth again, so I don't pull into the parking lot, but when I get back up on top of the hill on the other side of the valley, it starts cutting out again.

I pull into the parking lot at Pomponio State Beach to take a look, but what's the use? I don't have any tools with me, and I wouldn't know what to do with them if I had any. So, I take a quick look under the hood anyway and can't figure out what's wrong. I close the hood and continue my trip south. The car runs rough all the way to Arroyo de los Frijoles. Just as I round the corner where you can see Pigeon Point, I'm looking at a band of blue sky beyond the lighthouse. At the moment when I get to the Point, the car's engine starts running smoothly, and I'm driving under a clear blue sky.

The Ragman Draws Circles

Saturday, May 29, 1976

I

At nine o'clock I start packing my towels and getting ready to go downtown. I just took a couple rips from my pipe and I'm feeling pretty mellow. I put the towels in the laundry bag first. On top of them I put *Far Tortuga* and the loose-leaf binder with my card file. I pick up my appointment book and walk to the front of the garage. I unlock the garage door and go in to where I keep my bike parked. I put the appointment book in the basket first and put the laundry bag on top of it. I stretch the elastic cord over everything and push the bike out onto the driveway apron in front of the garage. Each step of the way is delayed because I keep thinking I've forgotten something, and every time I go to make a move, I hesitate and start to move in another direction. When I finally decide to close and lock the garage door, the phone rings, so I go back and answer it. I have an off-prem extension.

"Jerôme's hairstyles."

"Jerôme, this is Dave Raska."

"Hey, Dave. What's up?"

"I need a haircut."

"Today?"

"Sure, if I could."

"Okay, hold on. Got'a look at my book."

"Okay."

Jerome Arthur

I put the phone down, walk back out to the bike, and get the appointment book.

"Okay, Dave, this morning or this afternoon?"

"As early as possible."

"Okay. Let's make it ten this morning. That gives you about an hour."

"I'll see you then," he says and hangs up.

I hang up and write his name in the space marked ten o'clock. My only appointment all day. I'm knocking 'em dead today! I go back out to the bike and put the appointment book back into the basket and put the towels back in on top of it. I lock the garage door and look at the time on my pocket watch. It's nine o'clock sharp. I get on the bike and ride off down the street, heading away from the shop in downtown.

It's Saturday of Memorial Day weekend, and I'm go'n'a go all the way around today since the weather's so nice and I haven't ever really made the complete circle before. It's out of the way, but it'll make a good bike ride, and by the time I get to the shop, I'll be refreshed and feeling good, and maybe I'll be a little more enthusiastic about going to work. That's the nicest way I can say that I don't enjoy my job when I have to call it work. That's what happens whenever I'm cutting under someone else's roof, paying off his investment and not my own. See, that's how bad it's gotten since I moved my business to Santa Cruz. As recently as last year, I was saying that cutting hair isn't like work at all. Ella tells me to be patient, that someday soon I'll have my own shop again, like the one I had up in El Granada.

I have to admit though that my arrangement here is better than it was in the Shore, since here I'm renting a chair and down there I had to give Bernie thirty percent off the

178

One And Two Halves

top. At least here my rent doesn't go up just because I'm making more money. If I could only get as busy here as I was there. Not just with cutting hair, but with other things too, like the classes I used to take at City and State College. They kept me busier than I've ever been in my life. It seems all I was doing was going from home to school to work and home again without any side trips to the beach. I don't know why I did it. I look at my old lecture notes now and wonder why I found it so attractive. I probably wouldn't do it again, or at least I'd do it differently. I remember one time riding my bike in a driving rain to get to a final exam. I had to take my shoes and socks off when I got to class and wring the socks out like a dishrag. And for what? A grade. After the test was over and it was still raining, I hid out in the library, and if it didn't stop, I eventually rode to the shop in the downpour, and if it didn't stop raining before I got off at six, I rode home in it and in the dark too, unless I tried waiting it out at the bar across the street.

Those experiences seem so far away now as I pedal to an empty schedule except the half hour between ten and ten-thirty. The mailman is coming my way about a half block down the street on the other side. We wave as we pass each other. I wonder where he lives. Probably over in the Circles. That's the neighborhood where most of the black people in Santa Cruz live. He probably gets his haircut from that black guy in the shop on Errett Circle. He wears a short Afro. hairstyle. With the weather warming up, he'll probably be shaving his head pretty soon. It was shaved at the end of last summer when I closed my shop in El Granada and started cutting hair in Santa Cruz. I wish he'd let me cut it so I could get some practice working on that kind of hair. I've only done two black people in the seventeen years I've been in the business. The first one was when I was going to barber college in Los Angeles. I'll never forget it. The guy started for my chair, and I told him I'd never worked on that kind of hair and I wasn't sure I knew how.

"You'll do okay," he said. "I'll tell you if you start to mess up."

I remember the instructor saying something about "Colored hair" being just the opposite of Caucasian hair. He said to taper down the nape of the neck with the number two blade rather than up it like we were doing on white people's hair. So, the customer told me what he wanted and I did it as best I could. The style was called a *Quo Vadis*, which meant shaving the hairline across his forehead and around the temples with the straight razor. The second experience I had was up in El Granada, of all places. There was a black guy with an afro. who worked in the cable T.V. shop next door, and I cut his hair once. I shampooed it first and layered it wet just like I do Caucasian hair. It came out all right just like the first one, but I really didn't feel like I knew what I was doing. What I need is someone regular like the mailman, but then I'll probably never cut his hair.

I'm coasting down King Street, taking a left on Ladera Drive, and that brings me back out on King at the back of Linda Vista Shopping Center. I take another left and come out on Mission Street on the edge of town. Cars zip along on their way up and down the coast; semis rumble by on their way to the industrial area over by Natural Bridges. I suddenly have the urge to have a Lifesaver, so I turn in at Linda Vista Market and get off my bike. I lift the bike up onto the sidewalk in front of the store and park it next to the door. The clock above the butcher's counter says nine-eleven and a half, and it's quiet in the store. I walk to the candy counter and pick up a pack of Spear-O-Mint Lifesavers. There's one person ahead of me at the cash register. She's got a few

One And Two Halves

items down on the counter and is walking up and down the aisles picking up other things. I wait a while, and the clerk finally says,

"Here, let me ring that up for yuh. Looks like she's go'n'a be a while getting' everything she wants."

"Thanks," I say putting my money on the counter.

I pop a Lifesaver into my mouth and get back on my bike. Watching for a break in traffic, I cut across Mission Street and onto the sidewalk on the other side. I'm much more careful nowadays than I ever was down south. In fact, sometimes I think I'm lucky to even be alive after some of the close calls I had riding around the Shore. I used to ride home from the A.I. late at night, and half loaded to boot. I can even remember one time *walking* down Ocean in the night and almost getting hit by a car. I was weaving and staggering along a section that was under construction, and as I was skirting the flashing sawhorses, I was kind of out in the road. Off in the distance headlights were coming toward me. In my drunken state, I was belligerent enough to challenge the oncoming headlights to a game of chicken, but that was only momentary. I suddenly realized that there was a three-thousand-pound car behind them, and I quickly jumped into the shallow ditch at the side of the road. He swerved to miss me. It was just another one of the stupid things I did when I was young and dumb.

In the row of shops on my left, there's a restaurant, a bar, a card room and a barber shop. When I see barber shops like this one, I think of the short story "The Hunger Artist" by Franz Kafka. The barber isn't in there now. In fact, I can't remember when I've ever seen him. When I have, he's been staring forlornly out the front window as if pleading for attention, any attention at all, like the hunger artist in the story before an attendant with a broom sweeps him out. Even I,

181

who have put in my time waiting for customers in barber shops, wonder what he does in there, whose hair he cuts. If I don't see him in there, then for sure I haven't seen any customers in there either. I expect to come by here one day and find the place cleared out, empty, perhaps even already incorporated into one of the other businesses on either side.

I pull in at the gas station on the corner of Mission and Swift. The air and water hoses aren't sticking out of their little metal box next to the pumps, so I walk over to the attendant who's standing in the glass and metal cage in the middle of the inside island.

"What's with the air hose?" I ask him.

"I beg your pardon," he says sarcastically, coming out of the cage and pulling his keys to the end of his retractable metal tether.

"Where's the air hose?" I ask him again, not realizing at first that he's kidding with me.

"I beg your pardon," he says again, winking this time. When he finds the right key, he stoops down to the lock on the cover with the two holes in it. After he pulls the two hoses out of the box and replaces the cover, I take the air hose and put the nozzle on the tire valve. The gauge goes up to forty-five pounds, and I screw the cap back on the valve.

I hop back on and start off down Swift, crossing the street diagonally as I go. A yellow Porsche honks at me. It's Sean, the bartender at the Crow's Nest, so I wave and continue on my way. I tried for three months to get him in for a haircut, and now it seems he won't go anywhere else. In fact, he turned out to be a damn good customer, always leaving me a little something extra like a buck or two tip or a joint of some ass-kicking weed. One time before I started cutting his hair, I saw him down at the Lane and he stopped to offer me a couple hits. It was about 9:30 on a Saturday morning. He was on his way home from his girlfriend's house. I was on my way to the shop, and there wasn't even one appointment in my book like today, so I figured what the hell? Why not? He was paying me back for a couple weeks before when we ran into each other and I had some.

It's a nice day, which means the beach'll probably be pretty crowded later on. It's one of those Southern California kind of days, as much as there can be a Southern California day in this cold neck of the woods. Sometimes I dress warm against the cold fog in the morning, and by lunchtime, it's so hot I wish I was wearing cutoffs. Hell, down south I worked from March to November in cutoff Levis and leather sandals. Compared to this, the Shore was like a tropical paradise; however, Santa Cruz is like a tropical paradise compared to El Granada.

The first year I worked with Bernie, I'd go down to Alamitos Bay every afternoon after work and swim from the Shore to Naples. I could even keep up that routine into October, but since I've been living here, I've never been in the water. The few times I've been to these beaches, I've only been able to get my feet wet, and then after a couple minutes they start aching like my head aches after I eat ice cream too fast. In addition to the weather and the beaches, working for Bernie was good entertainment. Just watching him work the angles was a trip. One of those angles was using linen towels twice before throwing them into the laundry. That was before we started doing shampoo cuts, when we were doing neck shaves with the straight razor. He spelled it out to me at the beginning.

"Parlay them towels to save on the linen bill," he said.

That lasted until the first time I got caught using a damp towel on the next customer. He made a big deal out of the fact that I was only an apprentice. He was ready to report me to the state board when Bernie came back and calmed him down and walked at his side out the front door talking in low tones while he was shaking his fist and saying very loudly that I ought to be reported. The next day Bernie ordered Barbee paper towels from Don at the barber supply and that's what we used from then until we started doing shampoo cuts. It seems to me now that he'd tried the paper towels once before and rejected them saying, "They're strictly N.G.," meaning no good.

I'm heading down Swift Street toward West Cliff Drive. As I come down off the mound in the road where the railroad tracks run, a little car carrying two railroad men goes scooting along the track behind me. The dogs in the fenced yard of the warehouse on my right are lazing around in the morning sun. It's so clear straight ahead that I can almost see the tip of the Monterey Peninsula down at the end of the street. Once I get past the warehouse, I'm looking across an open field where the Wrigley's and Lipton's plants sit. Natural Bridges State Park is across the street from Lipton's. Above the trees in the park, white clouds drift southward. It's go'n'a be a great bike ride today, like some I had along the beaches in the Shore when it was clear enough to see Catalina. That wasn't often. Maybe no more than a few days a year in January.

In the distance the street and the trees down that way frame the two-tone blue of sky and ocean. A guy who's doing a brick façade on the front of his house is mixing mortar, and as I coast by, he looks up from his work and I nod in his direction, but he turns away. I pedal down the street.

I can't figure out why people around here are so aloof and standoffish, why they don't just smile and say hello. That's one big difference between Northern and Southern

184

One And Two Halves

California. In the north there are so many hip and cool people trying to impress everybody else with their hipness and coolness. It's hard to make friends because of the cliques. Down south folks seem laid back and casual, except when they get on the freeway.

I have to laugh when I think about Vic, a guy I did some vacation work for after I left Bernie, and his affair with a woman named Tina. That was before I got married and moved north. His affair with Tina was common knowledge around the shop. Sometimes I think even Vic's wife knew about it. She hung around the shop a lot, sweeping the floor, rearranging magazines and getting her hair cut. She was there at least three times a week to help clean up at the end of the day. It seems to me impossible that she didn't know; in fact, she probably hung around to see if she could catch him in the act. One day I was giving Vic a haircut and Tina stormed into the shop, tears welling up in her eyes. Vic's wife wasn't around. Tina walked up to him and threw a locket on a chain into his lap. Then she stood over him, her lower lip quivering.

"I wanted you to keep the locket, honey," Vic finally said.

"The memories will only break my heart," she said. "Why, Vic? You know how much you mean to me."

"I just can't handle it anymore. My old lady's getting suspicious. The pressure's getting to be too much."

"I've always tried to stay out of the way. I never minded playing second fiddle. Why couldn't we keep things like they were?"

Vic looked at me in the mirror and shrugged his shoulders as if he expected me to give him the answer he couldn't come up with. I kept cutting his hair acting like I didn't know what was going on. I couldn't believe what I

185

was hearing. She was young and beautiful, so why didn't she find herself a nice young guy to go with instead of an overweight middle-aged barber who was married and had kids?

"Look, Tina baby. I'll get in touch with you later and we can iron things out. Okay?" He was trying to get rid of her in case his wife came in, but she wasn't leaving. She stood over him pouting, and I'm sure he was feeling like a chump; I know I was. He had a sheepish look on his face as he dodged her eyes in the mirror. When I finished the cut, I asked him what he thought of it, and he turned to Tina and said,

"How do you like it, baby?"

"Why don't you ask your 'old lady,'" she said vindictively. Vic turned and looked at me as if to say, "What do I say to that?" But I just shrugged and said, "You asked for that one." Tina shook her head and started for the door, but Vic didn't say or do anything to stop her. Instead, he looked at me and said,

"I love her, Jerôme, Yuh know. I just can't be tied down with her. It's bad enough I'm tied down with my old lady."

I thought he was missing the point, but who was I to say anything, so I kept my mouth shut.

Moving right along here, I pass houses on my left and warehouses and businesses on my right. There's this gray house with a white picket fence where two dogs live. A black poodle lounges on the front door stoop, obviously pampered and spoiled, while a bigger dog of mixed breed is tethered to a tree in the side yard. The mutt runs back and forth only as far as his leash permits. His yard is plenty big, but he only has about twenty-five feet of it. The rest is planted in corn and artichokes and beans. His run is a semicircu-

186

lar trench worn into the ground around the tree. The dog probably would be happier if he could run all the way around the tree, but he can't because the tree stands next to a six-foot high redwood fence. Looks like it's been that way for quite a while.

Approaching Delaware Avenue, I get a whiff of resin coming from Haut Surf Shop on the corner. I turn right and head straight out toward Natural Bridges. In the year I've lived here, I've only taken this route a few times. I usually only go as far out as Almar Street, which is a regular neighborhood street with houses on both sides. This way there's a lot of open space and beautiful views.

The clouds have drifted farther south, but they're still over the field at Natural Bridges. One of them is shaped like a car. Now isn't that interesting. Yeah, there it is. The hood and the passenger compartment and the wheels. And it's all kind of slanted forward as if the car is going south at high speed. Kind of the way cartoonists do it in the comics. All this cloud needs is three horizontal lines shooting off the trunk and rear window.

I get over to the middle of the street as I ride between Intel and Lipton. I cross over and make my left at Swanton Boulevard. I'm going south again toward West Cliff Drive. Now the wooded field of Natural Bridges State Park is on my right. Drawing near the bend in Swanton, I pull up to the curb where I can gaze over the lichen-mottled redwood fence. I'd done this many times at Recreation Park in Long Beach on brisk fall evenings or chilly winter ones, contemplating "Stopping by Woods on a Snowy Evening" through the dappled fog that hung low among the trees and shrubs. This park isn't quite the same as Recreation Park, and the setting isn't quite as enchanting as the scene in the

187

poem, but it's refreshing to stop here and relax in the sun before making my way to that empty schedule. Now that I have a closer view, I see weeping willows hanging under the tall pines and eucalyptus I saw earlier from the distance. This is where the Monarchs come every fall and hang on the eucs. They look like blankets of butterflies draped over the trees.

Three boys are playing on a tire swing hanging from an oak tree. Their pecking order is well established. The biggest of the three dominates the swing, but he's not necessarily the toughest, though he acts the toughest and does the most bullying. The littlest one gets his turn by sheer guile. The middle-sized kid is getting the fewest turns on the swing. Since he's bigger than the littlest one, he gets on the swing by overpowering the small guy, and then he shies away from him as if he's afraid the little guy's go'n'a beat him up. It reminds me of when I was a little kid and was usually the man in the middle. Memories of my childhood make me uneasy.

I push off from the curb and ride down the street toward West Cliff. The sun is getting higher. Everything glistens around me. The spring air is crisp and clear. There's a guy walking on the other side of the street carrying a handbag. He's wearing cutoffs and dirty white tennis shoes, no socks, and he has a beard and long hair. A telephone repairman approaches him from the other direction, and the young guy with the handbag smiles and nods at him, but the phone man takes his pipe out of his mouth, turns his head and spits a yellow brown mass into the gutter beside him. Then as they pass each other, the phone man shakes his head in apparent disgust. The kid with the handbag walks on his way still smiling.

I round the bend in Swanton and see the deep blue ocean straight ahead. The breeze suddenly stiffens and cools.

188

One And Two Halves

Seeing the spectacular panorama in front of me makes me wish I was on a deserted island in the South Pacific or Caribbean. How nice that would be. But then isn't that where I am right now? I might as well be. For as many years as I've been riding bikes, somehow I can't get over the loneliness of it. Even when you're riding with someone else, it's not really like being with somebody because you've each got your own bike, and you have to ride mostly single file so one of you doesn't get hit by a car or truck.

A westerly gust hits me and dies down to a gentle breeze again as I cut across West Cliff Drive to the bike path. Getting myself pointed in the right direction on the bike path, I stop at the cliff's edge, resting one foot on the redwood rail fence. This is the first of many well-known local surf spots that I'll be passing in the next three miles. Locals call this one Natural Bridges, which is actually the official name of the beach and state park behind it. I don't see any surfers in the water here. From this vantage point, I can see white sails tattooed to the blue horizon to the southeast a little way out from the mouth of the yacht harbor. Due south, the mountainous Monterey Peninsula looms blue as cobalt against the baby blue sky. Over my right shoulder, Natural Bridges Beach warms in the morning sun. I can't see the bridges because the cliff's in the way, but I can see a portion of the beach, and its beige sand looks warm to me up here in the breeze. Directly below me there's a cove with a sandy beach submerged as the whitewater ebbs and flows. The tide is in. When it's not, I bet the beach stays dry. Almost directly in the center of the mouth of the cove, a huge flat column of rock juts up out of the swirling water. About fifteen sea birds are on top, cawing and preening in the morning sun. Routinely, small groups take off from the westside of the rock, fly a huge loop, and land on the eastside.

Jerome Arthur

I start to ride again. The wind's at my back, which will make this stretch from here to Steamer Lane the easiest part of the ride. It's like running downwind with a full spinnaker. There have been times when I've been coming from the other direction in the afternoon against the same wind. If it wasn't for the clicking of the rear sprocket and the squeaking of the seat under me, I'd swear I was tacking downwind along the nine-mile-long breakwater that encloses Long Beach and Los Angeles Harbors. Once when Hutch, Clint and I were out there on my catamaran, we decided to tie up to the small dock at the eastern end of the breakwater. We'd all had too much to drink by that time. We brought the boat around, tacking away from the dock. Then we came about and made a run straight for it. I had the tiller, but I was so drunk that when we reached the dock, I didn't have the presence of mind to come about, so we slammed into the dock, splintering the bowsprit. We all laughed like hell. We tied up to the dock and climbed up on the rocks and boulders of the breakwater to view the surf crashing up against it on the ocean side. When we got back to the boat, we found some line in the forward hatch and lashed the bowsprit so we could still do some sailing. We spent the rest of the afternoon cruising up and down on that glassy stretch of water twenty feet or so inside the breakwater. Skimming would be a better word for it since the wind was heavy over the top of the breakwater.

=I'm cruising down West Cliff Drive looking alternately to my right out at the ocean and to my left at the houses that line the street. The sun sparkles platinum and gold on the aquamarine surface of the ocean. The houses are much like beach houses in any of the small towns and villages along the California coast. Built close together, there are small cottages right next to large modern houses that

190

One And Two Halves

look to me like misplaced transplants out of some tract of custom houses in Orange County.

The surf suddenly breaks on the cliff below, and a huge jet of water shoots up through a blowhole. There's a loud WHOOSH and the water falls in droplets on the stone shelf below. Rounding a bend in the bike path, I see two two-story weathered wood houses straight ahead. Another curve to the right and I'm overlooking another small cove. Since this one cuts deeper into the cliff, there's a fairly good size sandy beach that remains above water even when the tide is in.

There's a good-looking woman with red hair wading in the surf wearing cutoff jeans and nothing on top, so I stop and watch her for a while. She's very pretty. Looks a little like a barber I worked with once named Diane. Like me, she tried to get into teaching school. Unlike me, she got into barbering *after* she quit teaching. I worked my way through college cutting hair. She interviewed for teaching jobs for three years and finally got discouraged and gave up. At the time she was looking, there were few jobs and a lot of teachers. She was the only barber I ever knew besides me who was a college graduate, and it doesn't surprise me that she couldn't get a teaching job. I went through the process myself. I knew all the stories. There was the time that she was a long-term substitute for another teacher, and when the other teacher decided to call it quits for good, they hired somebody else over Diane to take the job permanently. There was also the time the school district she was subbing in hired someone over her, illegally. They hired someone quietly without advertising the job, and when Diane squawked, they gave her an interview just to keep her quiet, but the job was already filled. The real corker was the time they called her in for an interview, and the guy who interviewed her called her later

191

that night and told her that she didn't get the teaching job, but would she be interested in another job selling encyclopedias or floor cleaner or something like that? She finally gave it up and got into cutting hair. And she was a hell of a good barber, too. That's why I know she was probably a good teacher. I wonder whatever happened to her.

The red head on the beach looks up at me indifferently and moves off under the cliff where I can't see her. Too bad. I was just beginning to enjoy myself. I turn my handlebars straight and start pedaling down the bike path again. To my left is a green cottage with a white picket fence around it. Next to the driveway hanging on an inverted L made of redwood four by fours is a plaque of wood with a painting of a whale in the water. On the other side, there's a painting of a pelican in flight with a small fish in its beak.

The path is starting to straighten out now as I come up on San Jose Avenue where there's a small beach, and there are four surfers like shiny black corks on tongue depressors bobbing on the water about a quarter mile out. I pull up to the redwood rail fence and stop to watch them. Locals call this break Stockton Avenue. That's the next street ahead.

Sitting on top of the fence and down a way from me are two guys apparently talking about the waves and the swell. I can't hear them over the crashing of the surf. They're pointing out at the surfers and carrying on like they know what they're talking about. The ocean is flat except for a slight swell and some ripples caused by the breeze. The rim of the horizon forms a hoop. Straight ahead way off in the distance, I get my first glimpse of Seal Rock. I can't see the lighthouse yet from this vantage point. Maybe it'll come into view around the next bend. Way over across the bay I can see the P.G.&E. plant at Moss Landing, white smoke billowing silently from its stacks into the blue sky. The

192

One And Two Halves

clouds have drifted quite a ways south now, leaving the sky almost completely blue. The surf isn't very good right now. One of the guys down the way shouts,

"Not bad. Go for it," over the low roar of the ocean through his cupped hands.

A wave is coming up beyond the farthest surfer out. He lies down on his board and paddles diagonally across it. As it rises to its crest, he sits up on his board, points the nose of the board up, gets back on his stomach and starts digging. The crest of the wave catches him and he stands up on his board coming down the face of the wave. It's at this point that his board seems to drop and almost lose contact with his feet, but he stays on. When the wave breaks, he goes into the tube and rides it out till it's all whitewater, and then he sits down on the board again, turns around, lies on his stomach and paddles out of the whitewater and back to the outside. By now another wave is breaking and the guy who's trying to ride it wipes out. His board springs nose first out of the water and his head comes bobbing up behind it. The third wave in the set breaks much farther out and nobody gets a ride on it.

I've got that ten o'clock appointment, so I better get going. Appointments! Sometimes I think the world would stop turning without them. We have appointments to get our hair cut, our teeth drilled, and our cars lubed. Stores and shops keep regular hours; restaurants take reservations. Next thing you know, we'll have to have an appointment to get our share of oxygen, and if we don't keep that appointment, it'll be over. And for some folks, it gets over too soon.

Take Stan Toscano, for example. His shop was the last one I worked in for commission. I was on his payroll. He was withholding income tax and Social Security from my weekly take. When I left him, I opened up the first shop I ever owned in El Granada. Poor Stan. His appointment with the grim reaper came way too soon. Nobody gets out alive but he was too young.

Stan was one of the funniest guys I've ever known. He had a small library of pornographic movies that he rented out of his back room as a sideline. He never charged me anything, though, always laying one on me for an evening if I wanted it. He operated a fireworks concession out of that same back room every year around the fourth of July. One time the cops came in and hassled him. They said they'd caught a kid firing off an M80 in the Safeway parking lot and that he told them he'd gotten it from Stan. Stan told the cops he hadn't sold any to kids, but he admitted selling them, and if the fathers wanted to give their kids fireworks, he couldn't help it. Since he didn't have any incriminating evidence in the back room, they didn't arrest him or even cite him, but that little brush with the law didn't stop him. He was just more careful who he sold them to after that.

The first Christmas I worked with him, he had a bar set up in the back room. He had fifths of bourbon, scotch and tequila. The shop was a walk-in shop, no appointments, and every customer who came in was offered a drink. Of course, the customers didn't want to drink alone. They'd insist on our joining them. We would, and by the end of the day (Christmas Eve, no less), we were so drunk we couldn't cut straight lines if we had to.

Stan got killed in a motorcycle accident. The story I got from his widow was that he'd already left his house to drive the car to work, but when he got to the front of Linda Mar Valley, it was still sunny and he figured it would stay that way all the way to Pacific Manor. She said he told her when he got back to the house how nice the weather was, and he wanted to take his Harley instead of the car. That was

194

One And Two Halves

the last time she spoke to him. I don't know why I think about these things now. I'm guessing maybe it's because I'm looking out at the immensity of this ocean and realizing how insignificant we humans are in this universe.

I'm coasting down the hill to the hairpin turn where Stockton Avenue intersects West Cliff Drive. The sprawling coastline arcs to my right, and for the first time, I can see the lighthouse at Steamer Lane. The point tapers down into the water and emerges again at a little distance forming Seal Rock, which is a perfectly symmetrical half-disc (at this distance) on the water's surface. I can neither see nor hear the seals barking from here. Directly below me and straight ahead is a huge rock outcropping that forms a low shelf at water's edge. Its pock-marked surface serves as tide pools for sea life when the tide is out. Looking up, I see more of these formations to as far as the house sitting on the cliff on the ocean side of the street at Fair Avenue.

A jogger approaches and as she gets closer, I can see she's not half bad. Her black Lab, his pink tongue hanging out, trails along behind her with that crooked gait that dogs have. Whenever I see a dog cantering that way, I think of Jonesy, the barber Bernie used to get for relief when he took a vacation. Jonesy wasn't a bad barber; he was just a stone alkie. He'd gone to barber school back in the forties and twenty years later, he still only had an apprentice license. He lived with his mother and as far as I know, he never moved out on his own or got married. He was a mama's boy all his life. Seeing the dog makes me think of Jonesy because when he used to walk down Second Street half loaded, his hunch back rising up to the sky (he was about six feet three inches tall and skinny as a rail), he sauntered along as crooked as an Irish Setter. Even his hipbones stuck out like a Setter's; his baggy pleated trousers hung crooked from them, held up by galluses. I used to watch the guy cut hair and if he was sober, he was sweating bullets and shaking like a dog shitting peach pits, but if he'd had a couple belts, he was as smooth as the next guy. The only problem was he couldn't just settle for a couple belts. He'd have to have a pint before lunch, and then he'd be no good for the rest of the day. If he's still alive, I'll bet he's still living with his mother in the Shore and still drinking like a fish.

To my right over by the edge of the cliff there's a sign on a wooden post. It says: DANGEROUS CLIFFS & WATERS/NO OVERNIGHT STAYS ORD. 13.12, and just below it on the post is one of those yellow warning signs that has a picture of a guy suspended in midair falling off a cliff. Big chunks of the cliff are suspended with him.

I'm passing Swift Street on the left. This whole block of West Cliff could have been transplanted here from Seal Beach, or from any Southern California beach town I've ever been in for that matter. Weathered wood, nets and shells festooned on railings of decks, an old rowboat marooned on a pile of sand in a front yard, seagull decoys perched on dock pilings, shingled verandas, a battleship gray cottage with white trim, stucco and red tile mansards with wrought iron deck railing that looks like coat hanger wire from this distance. The ocean crashes against the cliff where the white house with the guest cottage next to it faces the weather on the cliff's edge.

Aw, Seal Beach. A girl I dated for a while at City College said she always wanted to live there. That's probably a major reason why I didn't marry her. I wasn't into that kind of lifestyle. I was twenty-three and pretty conservative; she was only nineteen and to my way of thinking at the time, an incurable romantic. She wore flowers in her shoulder length black hair and billowy dresses that wafted in the breeze when she came to me. At the time Seal Beach was a haven for beats, flower children and other assorted counter-culture types. Hippies came five years later. I was just starting to make some money cutting hair, and I also wanted to get my college education. I was more of a student beach bum than a bohemian. Her friends were aspiring poets, actors and folk singers who lived in Seal Beach; mine were students, beach people and bar flies from Belmont Shore. It seems like the only time we weren't against each other was when we were in bed, but even then we were cast in traditional male/female roles of hunter and prey. What a time it was to be alive and in love! If I ever saw her walking down the street with another guy, it would break my heart. I know she loved me, but I was broken-hearted anyway when I saw her with other guys. When I think about it, I guess I'm lucky I didn't marry her. She was really only the kind you fall in love with, like Colina in "El Paso."

Since I got onto West Cliff, I've had a steady view of the smokestacks at the P.G.&E. plant across the water at Moss Landing. To the right of the plant, there is an enormous gap in the mountain, the end of the Salinas Valley where the Salinas River flows to the bay. The land mass to the right of the gap, from Marina to the Monterey Peninsula, looks like an island. Different shades of blue mark the various ridges on the side of the mountain. It kind of reminds me of San Bruno Mountain on the southern edge of San Francisco.

Once when I was working with Stan, he and I went cruising around up in Colma. We'd taken our shears up to get sharpened from an old German who had a shop on Valencia near 16th Street in the City. It was on the way home that Stan decided to take the run through Colma. Anybody who's familiar with San Francisco, knows it's where all the

197

graveyards and cemeteries are. Wyatt Earp is buried up there. We were driving along when we approached a rise, and as we came to the top, we could see a cemetery directly below us with all its tombstones in straight lines, erect and neat, and beyond it lay the rows of houses like headstone necklaces around the hill across the valley in Daly City. Monterey is a little too far away from here to see the kind of detail that we saw that day, but it's a similar scene because of the crystal clearness of the day.

The house on the cliff is just ahead to my right. It obliterates the view as I pass it. It's a white wood house in the style my wife calls Pennsylvania Dutch, but someone else told me that those tipped ends of the roof ridges are Tudor hips. The two dormers facing the street have regular peaked gables. There's a small cottage built next to it—kind of a guest house.

It looks like whoever lives there now is using it for his work because he has a drafting table set up in the huge picture window that looks into the Pacific sunset. I've often thought it would be a nice place to have a barber shop. I could live in the house and work in the cottage. No commute time, and I'd have a great view. Both structures have stone chimneys. I could get a cord of wood for the rainy season and build a fire every day. On days like this, I could be wearing cutoffs and sandals instead of button-down and oxfords. It would be nice all right, but I bet the city wouldn't go for it.

I meet the sun again on the other side of the trees beyond the house to the northeast. To my right and some twenty miles across the water is the Monterey Peninsula and Salinas Valley. Directly in front of me stands a huge symmetrical cypress tree with its roots clawed into the cliff, the surf rushing in and out at its talons. More tide pools are just below it.

198

One And Two Halves

My wife takes out-of-town guests down there on field trips. That sounds like I'm joking but it's true. Whenever people are visiting from out of town, she goes into her teacher mode and becomes their tour guide. She shows them West Cliff Drive, the University and downtown. The tide pools tour on West Cliff is one of her favorites. Once I went on one, and I was really impressed. Even from the tide pool shelf and the sandy beach underneath it, the cypress tree is unusually symmetrical. The symmetry of the massive root structure matches the tree's huge evergreen branches swaying in the azure breeze.

I'm coming up on Almar Avenue, closer to where I usually pick up the bike path. This is a well-known local surf spot called Mitchell's. Up ahead the old guy with gray hair I've seen around here before is walking in my direction. He looks like he's sick and dying. Every time I see him, his physical appearance seems to have deteriorated since the time before. He has a faraway look in his eyes. He strolls along the bike path taking in the ocean and the fresh air. The shelf with the tide pools is just opposite of where Almar lets out onto West Cliff.

The surfers around here have names for all these little coves and points. I've mentioned Natural Bridges and Stockton Avenue or Merced depending on who you talk to. Right here is Mitchell's. Coming up are Finger Bowl at the foot of Woodrow, Its Beach and Steamer Lane on either side of Lighthouse Point. Indicators and Cowell's are up by the Dream Inn. The last three are the breaks where the regular board surfers go. Boogie boarders go to Finger Bowl and Its Beach. Sometimes there are surfers here at Mitchell's, but not very often. There are rocks out there and usually the

199

waves aren't very good, but when the surf is good, the locals will be out at this spot. Right now, there's no surf here.

This section of the bike path is open and straight, so I'm rolling along at a pretty good clip. I come out from under the shade of the cypress tree and start a gently sloping uphill ride. Up ahead where the bike path bends slightly to the east, there's no one walking or riding for the half mile or so that I can see. Across the street to my left, a man with Down Syndrome makes an attempt at mowing his lawn. He stops mowing and starts talking and gesturing to the lawn mower. It reminds me of the Down Syndrome man who lived in the neighborhood I grew up in. What the hell was his name? I used to see him around town all the time, talking to a lamp post or parking meter. One time I saw him talking to a gas pump at the Flying A station, and I stopped to listen to what he had to say, but his speech was no more intelligible than Ike Snopes's. Ah, I remember his name now. It was Bart.

The bike path bends where Almar and Sunset come into West Cliff. In the triangle formed by those three streets is a rundown old pink house with windows looking out at the ocean. Dusty, twisted cypress trees mark the boundary of the property, blocking the view from the house. Another big cypress tree (but not as big or symmetrical as the one back by the tide pools) stands on the edge of the cliff to my right. A fishy smell rises from the kelp and debris scattered on Mitchell's Beach. Black swarms of gnats and flies emerge from the seaweed, disturbed by a dog chasing a stick its owner has thrown.

Across the water, now ripply, now smooth as glass, marking air currents, the ever-present mountain stands poised against the blue sky. Small waves break on the sand

200

One And Two Halves

below, a contrast from the booming assault of the surf on the sheer cliff back down the road a bit. Three pelicans glide in a triangle no more than a foot above the surface of the water.

I begin to coast down another hill, the one that goes down to a bridge over a gully next to Woodrow Avenue where a creek bed lets out onto a small beach. This is Finger Bowl. The beach is only a beach at low tide. Right now it's a medium tide and only half submerged. I start pumping hard to get enough steam to go up the other side. It reminds me of when I was a kid in Los Angeles. They were laying a new sewer down the center of Colorado Boulevard, the main drag in the old neighborhood of Eagle Rock. The pipe was probably five or six feet in diameter, and we used to go up into it while they were still putting it in. We'd go as far as we dared before it got too dark and we got scared, and then we'd ride our Flexies down, going up the sides of the pipe the whole way. Nowadays I guess the kids would do the same thing only with skateboards.

When I cross the bridge at the bottom of the hill, I look straight up Woodrow Avenue, and I can see the cross of the Garfield Park Church. It's in the center of some streets that form circles (in fact, they're called "The Circles") expanding outward—Errett Circle, Wilkes Circle, and Walk Circle—like the ripples in a pond after a pebble splashes on the surface. The scene passes by swiftly, and I bear down on the pedals. Shifting into fourth gear about two thirds of the way up the hill, I look over to my right where the cliff has again become abrupt and there's a narrow cove at the bottom.

Once before when I was riding by here, I stopped and climbed down the cliff to the cove. Because it's so narrow when you're down there, all you can see is water and, on a clear day like today, the land mass across the bay, and

201

all you can hear is the ocean. No houses, no cars, no streets, no power and telephone lines. Your point of view is completely different when you're down there; in the absence of the familiar remnants of civilization, you're in a perfect wilderness. When I used to live in Belmont Shore, I would walk out to the end of the west jetty at the mouth of Alamitos Bay and climb down the rocks where I could sit close to the surface of the water. If I faced the right direction, I couldn't see all the familiar signs of the mass of civilization behind me. It's not like that today. Now there's a huge oil platform a ways off from the Seal Beach Pier. Over on the Long Beach side, there's the breakwater, of course, but now there's always a tanker or two inside it.

Reaching the top of the hill, I shift back into fifth gear, and since I'm coasting now, I look at my pocket watch. It's nine thirty-two. Another stretch of road like the Seal Beach of about fifteen years ago is coming up. Gray and white cottages with glassed-in sun porches and stone chimneys, split a couple of vacant lots. Beige stucco two stories with pitched red tile roofs, and the ever present transplanted tract house also appear in this block.

Columbia Street is coming up. The first time I ever rode this bike path, I got on it here. That was last September when I finally started renting a chair in the shop I'm cutting in now. The bike path wasn't even paved this far. The pavement stopped at Pelton Street where Marello Prep faces the surf at Indicators and the Lane. From Pelton all the way out to Natural Bridges it was all gravel back then.

Sails come into view just opposite Seal Rock. The same ones I saw back up the road. Seems a bit early in the morning to be out sailing. Although, there *is* a slight breeze. It doesn't usually come up till afternoon. Two white ones and a red one. They're too far out for me to tell what class

202

One And Two Halves

they are. They're monohulls. I can see that much. One of
'em looks like a day sailor. I can't tell if the guys sailing it
are wearing wet suits. I bet they are; otherwise they're freez-
ing their noojies off. Below me, the slap-and-clap of a breaking wave against a rock, the hissing of the whitewater. Two
condo complexes are on the corner of Columbia and West
Cliff separating Columbia from Lighthouse Field.

There's a section of redwood rail fence right here, so
I pull up for my last look at the view in peace and quiet.
Once I get to the point, it's go'n'a start to get crowded, especially if there's any swell at all. From this side of the point it
looks pretty good. Bird Rock is off to my right. It's a flat
rock maybe fifteen/twenty feet away from the cliff measur-
ing something like twenty feet long and about eight feet
wide. It's obvious that not too long ago, it was connected to
the cliff by a natural bridge. There must be fifty pelicans
perched on it right now, and they take off in small groups
from one side, fly a loop and land on the other side. Above
the steady crashing of the surf, the sea lions are barking out
on Seal Rock and basking in the morning sun.

I push off and cruise unhurriedly in third gear along
the southern perimeter of Lighthouse Field. When I get to
the Point, I'll be halfway around the circle I'm riding in. It'll
also be the point at which I make my sharpest turn.

I can see the Dream Inn through the trees in the
Field. I'll be there in just a couple minutes. Lighthouse Field
is a big piece of wilderness right here in town. It has mead-
ows, thinning stands of Monterey cypress and eucalyptus,
and there's even an overgrown, marshy bird habitat. This is
another spot that the monarchs like to come to. It's about a
half mile long by about a quarter mile wide. I saw an aerial
photo once over at the bank of this whole stretch of land tak-
en maybe fifty years ago. It was before the lighthouse was

built and the field looked like a forest. There must've been a hundred times as many trees as there are now. The traffic has taken its toll on the tree population in the subsequent years since the picture was taken. Now all that remains are a few scattered cypress and eucs. and some scrawny looking underbrush. Most of the trees that survived look like they're going the way of their brethren; some are mere ghosts of trees already with bare broken limbs hanging from bare gray trunks.

The field has been a political football over the years. Not long ago some developers wanted to put in a convention center/shopping center complex, but local environmentalists and surfers got together and raised so much hell about it that they backed off. Then the state and local governments were supposed to buy it and make it into a regional park, but I don't know whatever happened to that plan. The field still lies dormant and idle, blighted as recently as last year by people who camped there in old school busses, motor homes and vans. Surfers and tourists park their cars there. When some of those people became permanent residents, "No Trespassing" signs, backed up by government ordinances, were posted, and the cops were coming around at night and rousting out anybody who was violating them. It seems to have helped, but more needs to be done. I'd be in favor of closing the whole area off to motor traffic from Pelton to Columbia, but that'll never happen.

The green grass of the field rushes by on my left. The wind has stiffened slightly. Down below on my right, people are running their dogs on Its Beach. The specter of the doomed cypress trees in Lighthouse Field pervades the scene. There are rickety old wooden benches built into the ridge along the western-facing cliff of Lighthouse Point. They provide a perfect seat for watching the sun set.

One And Two Halves

Suddenly, I hear skidding tires screech behind me, and when I look around, a black dog cowers under the wheels of a Capri and runs off into the shelter of the field while the driver bellows obscenities at him. Beat up, surf-board-laden Volkswagens pass shiny Volvos and B.M.W.s on West Cliff Drive.

The traffic increases noticeably. The gravel path that encircles the lighthouse forks off to the right. I turn onto it. The lighthouse parking lot is about half filled with cars. A few have empty surfboard racks on top. People are strolling out to the point. I head out around the lighthouse to the cliff where I can watch the surfers at the Lane. The breeze stiffens momentarily and lets up as I pass the windward side of the lighthouse.

The lighthouse is a monument to a young kid who died out here in a boating accident. When I was new in town, I went inside once to check it out. There was a bronze plaque with a dedication from the father to the dead son. I can't even remember their names now. They're probably prominent old timers from around here.

When I come to the path that leads out to the end of the point, I turn left to go over by the cliff where I can see the surfers close up. The path straight ahead leads out to the end of the point where there's a closer look at the sea lions on Seal Rock, but I've been out that way before and I think I know the seals well enough; what I've got'a do is get acquainted with some of these surfers, who will sooner or later be needing haircuts. I pull up next to a coin operated telescope, put my feet down and, straddling my bike, I watch the surfers jockeying for position.

This is Steamer Lane, the best point break in Santa Cruz, maybe even the best in California. There are a couple small groups of people and a few individuals milling around

205

near the edge of the cliff. A gray-haired old surfer I've seen around here before is surrounded by a group of young tow-heads. They're passing a joint around; the old man isn't smoking with them. He's telling them about the biggest wave he ever rode, which was up near the mouth of the Columbia River where Washington and Oregon meet. The kids around him are alternating exclamations, "Yeah!" "Wow!" "Outa' sight!" "Ri'lly!" "Fur sure!" "Right on!"

He must have seen a pretty big wave recently, from the look of it. He's leaning on a pretty sturdy cane.

The surfers bob up and down in the water below, waiting for a wave. The aging surfer cups his hands and hollers out to them, "Number two!" There's a set coming up and he's telling them to catch the second wave in the set.

From here you can really see how they're coming up. Like the stages of a person's life. You have to look back to see them. When I think of the stages I've been through, I can hardly believe it all happened. Just the changes I've been through in barbering alone. At one time I scheduled appointments in big blocks of time on different days. I might work from nine to two on Wednesday and from one to six on Thursday and back in the morning on Friday and Saturday. The first couple shops I worked in were walk-in shops. It wasn't until I went to work for Bernie that I even started scheduling appointments, and it took us five years to start doing it. We took them as they walked in the door when I started with him. A rolling motion developed, like the swell. I'd get used to various busy times during the day and even the busy days of the week. It only seems like lately that the rolling motion has slowed. I'm afraid it might stop like maybe today at one name in the book.

The set produced three pretty good waves. About six guys got good rides. On the last wave, one poor bastard got

One And Two Halves

stuck on the inside in all the whitewater. He's still trying to paddle out, and each time another wave breaks, he gets battered back, so he's losing more ground than he's gaining. The aging surfer and his young cronies are recounting the three waves—how good they were, what kind of rides the surfers got, how they would have ridden them.

I get back on the path and start pedaling. As I come around to the other side of the parking lot, I'm back on the bike path just a few feet from where I got off it on the other side of the lighthouse. Once back on the path, I'm heading east northeast.

The sun flashes off the surface of the water in a dazzling array of gold drops that make me squint. The two sides of the lighthouse are like two different worlds. Just a few minutes ago I was in a wilderness of ocean on one side and the field on the other. Now I'm in traffic that rivals the downtown Mall. Empty beer cans and crumpled cigarette wrappers are scattered about. Dumpsters are filled to the brim on the edge of the field. The traffic has slowed; the drivers look at the scenery. There must be fifteen pedestrians in front of me on the bike path, some surfers carrying their boards, some tourists and dog walkers. The trees are dustier and more ragged on this side of the field than on the other side. I forge my way forward past the wooden stairs that lead down to the water. A large wooden sign next to the stairs says:

TRADITIONAL RULES OF SURFING

PADDLE AROUND WAVE NOT THROUGH IT
FIRST SURFER ON WAVE HAS RIGHT OF WAY
HANG ONTO YOUR BOARD
HELP FELLOW SURFER

Jerome Arthur

BY SAM REID

CITY OF SANTA CRUZ
PARKS & RECREATION

As soon as I get past the steps, the foot traffic seems to thin out, but not the car traffic. The parking spaces in the turnout along the cliff are all occupied, and cars are parked all along the curb and around the dusty edge of the Field forming what looks like a huge broken smile. Posting the rules of surfing is like posting speed limit signs without having cops to enforce them, or like trying to keep everything according to Hoyle in a game of canasta. I've heard card table chatter before, and I've heard surfers hollering obscenities at each other for getting in the way.

"I meld and that way Myrtle has the responsibility to pass the pile on to Jenny."

"Hey, you son of a bitch! Watch where you're go-in'!"

"Okay, Jenny, that's it! I hope everyone played their shtick." The cards go *"flap, flap"* in their suits and pairs on the table.

"Number two! Go left. Ah, he got stuck on the in-side."

"I have absolute garbage."

"It's only because you have six, fives, fours. Right?"

"No. I'm go'n'a give it to you."

"Look at this! I'm go'n'a go for it."

Rounding the bend around the turnout, I come to another slope. Since I turned at the point, the pier is stretched out on the water in front of me. From this distance the pilings look like little black match sticks. The blue landmass

208

One And Two Halves

across the water is in full view from Cypress Point on the right to the Wharf straight ahead. As I look at the mountain on the left side of the Salinas Valley behind Moss Landing, I notice that the jagged ridge is almost symmetrical, two points on each side of a quarter round summit. That's twice this morning that I've seen symmetry in nature.

The crowds have thinned noticeably since I left the Point, but that'll change shortly. Up ahead at Indicators there's another turnout parking area with cars in all the spaces, and people are shuffling about by the iron bar fence at the edge of the cliff. I've always wondered why they put a parking area there. It's in a dangerous bend in the road.

I'm doing another one of those down-and-ups, and as I get to the top on the other side, I'm at Pelton Street. I look to my left straight down the street and see a blue V of sky plunge into the street in the distance. Another spoke in the wheel. Swift, Fair, Almar, Woodrow, Columbia, and now Pelton. Next is Bay, the last spoke. Not to mention Santa Cruz and Monterey Streets between here and there. Marello Prep. and Saint Joe's Shrine Catholic Church are on my left, and I'm seeing the last of Lighthouse Field. This is Indicators, the spot where I met Sean that other Saturday morning when we smoked a number together. Business was slow then, and it's still slow now. This is the toughest town I've ever tried to build a business in. It's been eight months, and it's still slow. It didn't take me that long in El Granada, and I was busy on the first day I stepped into Bernie's shop in the Shore. I can hardly believe I've only got one haircut scheduled today. The other barbers I work with are plenty busy, but then they've been cutting hair here for a long time.

The next quarter mile or so of road bends into an S shape. I've rounded the bottom part of it, and now I'm going almost due north. In just a couple minutes I'll be going northeast along Cowell's Beach, and then due east when I get to Beach Street at the Dream Inn. The Wharf and the Boardwalk to my right are gangly skeletons along the eastern horizon. The Dream Inn, a concrete box with a green and red neon Di at its crest, is the town's only high-rise. Cowell's beach stretches along a cove that's sheltered from the open ocean.

I feel more in the city when I compare these houses to the ones on the other side of the Field. This neighborhood's got concrete curbs, gutters and sidewalks. The houses along here are close together, the lawns neatly manicured, though some are not. They seem generally better taken care of than the ones on the other side of Lighthouse Field. The city is taking a little better care of the cliff side of the street here, too. On the other side of the Field, tall weeds shoot up amid the ice plant that grows from the edge of the cliff to the bike path. Here the city maintains planters in the turnout, and they keep the weeds mowed and edged along the bike path. The fence rails on the other side were all redwood, which did look kind of rustic; here they're all tubular steel painted blue green. Very slick.

The surf here is long and rolling like how I remember it at Waikiki. The crashing is muted because it's so far away and it's small, like Waikiki. The wind is still coming from the southwest, but the houses on my left are serving as a break, so I'm not getting much of a push from it like I got coming around the Point. This section of beachfront really reminds me of that stretch of Ocean Boulevard between Redondo and Cherry in Long Beach. Classy.

On my right down on the cliff below the bike path, there's a concrete building that houses two restrooms. Its flat roof is almost level with the bike path. Above it is another Traditional-Rules-of-Surfing sign. As I pass the sign, I look

One And Two Halves

back at the other side of it and read, "VALLEY GO HOME" in huge white painted letters. The same saying is painted in black spray on the roof of the building below. Here there's another iron rail fence keeping guard over a dirt trail leading down to the cove, which is directly below me. Down on the trail standing up close to the concrete wall foundation of the fence is a guy pissing up against the wall. What a jerk! All he had to do was go a few more steps to the toilet in the concrete building.

Some teenagers are milling around an open van at the parking turnout at Sharpe Overlook. I get a whiff of what they're smoking when I go by. It sure smells good. It wouldn't be bad if I could stop and have a toke or two, but even if I knew them and could stop, I've still got that ten o'clock appointment to keep. On the cliff by the turnout, there's a boulder with a bronze plaque on it in front of a wooden sign. The plaque on the boulder is inscribed with the legend:

BRUCE L. SHARPE OVERLOOK
PRESENTED TO THE CITY OF SANTA CRUZ
BY
MAUDE B. SHARPE
IN MEMORY OF HER HUSBAND
BRUCE L. SHARPE
NOVEMBER 19, 1963

The routed letters of the wooden sign are painted yellow.

SHARPE OVERLOOK
CITY OF SANTA CRUZ
PARKS & RECREATION DEPT.
DANGEROUS CLIFFS & WATERS

211

Jerome Arthur
NO OVERNIGHT STAYS ORD. 13.12

The road bends just beyond the turnout forming the top of the S, and now the bike path begins to narrow and four pine trees clumped on the edge of the cliff ahead obscure the road. Rounding the top bend in the S, a jogger is running by the trees. I can see that by the time I catch up to him, we'll be in the narrowest section of the bike path where it'll be hard to get around him, and he's running right in the middle. I'll have to slow down until the path gets wider and I can get around him. At Dutra Overlook I begin to pass, and as I get abreast of him, he turns his head slightly my way and is startled by my presence. He shouts at my back,

"Hey asshole! Say something?" but I ignore him.

Damn pedestrians! Why in hell don't you keep right?

Bay Street is coming up on my left and the Dream Inn on my right. I've seen my last real view of the water. It'll come up again when I get down on Beach Street, but it'll be a low view tunneled by the Wharf on one side and East Cliff on the other. The boarded-up windows of the old abandoned Sisters Hospital on the corner of Bay and West Cliff are blind to the view that isn't anymore because of the Dream Inn and the Sea and Sand Motel. Wildflowers bloom in the vacant lot on the other corner. I get a quick glimpse of the beach and Boardwalk below and then I start down the hill where the road forks. Coasting beside a bronze Maverick full of people, I hear the distant sound of a train whistle. At the bottom of the hill, I get over near the curb next to a green Triumph about to make a right. The driver is a pretty good-looking young lady. A husky guy with a deep tan is in the passenger seat. I slow down a little at the stop sign and begin to advance straight ahead as the Triumph makes its turn. The

212

One And Two Halves

girl catches sight of me just in time and hits her brakes. She stops within inches of my front wheel. The guy hollers,

"Hey, asshole! You're supposed to stop at the sign. Watch where the hell you're going!"

He's right. What can I say? So, I don't say anything. I move forward through the intersection, and they make their right. He's still hollering something at me, but it's lost in the din of traffic. I hear the train whistle again louder as I pass the Ideal Fish Company on the beach next to the wharf. The temperature seems to have gone up a degree or two since I came down the hill, and the wind isn't so bad down here. People are sunning on the motel decks above the shops across the street. There are only a few sunbathers scattered on the beach, but I bet this beach will be packed in a couple hours. The train whistle goes off again, this time really loud. The blare ceases the instant the locomotive pokes its massive nose around the corner of the Cocoanut Grove up ahead. Its one light shines brightly, almost outshining the brilliance of the day. I get up on the sidewalk and continue on my way. I count the cars as the train goes by: five box cars, five sand cars, a caboose and the engine and tender. Thirteen in all. It's on its way up to the cement plant in Davenport. I hear one final blast of the whistle and the train with all its rumbling and clacking is gone. The last I hear of the train is a distant wail of its whistle from the other side of Neary Lagoon. I've reached the Casino. The neon-tubed clock inside says nine forty-seven.

I should start hustling to get to work, and what better place to hurry past. It's Memorial Day weekend and the Boardwalk's go'n'a be busy. The parking spaces are filling up rapidly and the people are streaming into the Boardwalk. Some of the amusements are already open. I want to get out of this as quickly as I can. At the Sun Shops there's a driveway going back down to the street, so I cross the tracks and go down. Threading my way through traffic, I get to the other side and I make my left at Riverside Avenue. Here the traffic is thick and fast, so I'm moving along at probably ten miles an hour. I want to get out of it. A couple Mexican kids come out of the store at the corner of Riverside and Leibrandt and cross the street in front of me. After slowing down so I don't hit them, I cross Second Street and angle to the left up Leibrandt shifting into second gear as I climb the small hill that leads to Laurel Street Extension along the river.

  This neighborhood is a strange mixture of seedy cottages, Victorians, restored and not, and some fairly respectable looking motels with swimming pools. There's a kind of grandeur about a Victorian, even when it's in disrepair and run down. When South Central Los Angeles became a slum, and the beautiful rambling mansions of the area were converted into apartment houses by slum landlords, the architecture endured. It told the passing world it would prevail in spite of the kind of junk that had sprung up around it. This run-down old Victorian on my right is like that. Too bad whoever owns it doesn't take better care of it. The three-foot high weeds all around it don't add to its character.

  I start my left turn onto Laurel Street Extension, keeping a close eye out for traffic. This is probably the most dangerous part of my ride. The road is narrow and winding, and if a car comes in either direction, I've really got to watch out. If no cars come, everything's cool and I can ride right through with no hassle. Just for kicks, I think I'll take the bike path along the levee. I pull onto it where it rises to the level of the street. I start to pedal along toward the Broadway Bridge when I see a group of guys, two on each side of the bike path facing each other, hanging around right where the

One And Two Halves

bike path goes under the bridge. "PUNK!" is painted in big white letters on the side of the bridge over the bike path. Suddenly a sense of impending danger floods over me. I don't know what it is exactly, but the feeling is ominous. A couple of them have scruffy beards and they all look pretty scuzzy, but what can you tell by a person's looks? I'm not going that way. I turn my bike around and head back toward the street. Damn, what the hell is this, Haight/Ashbury? Well, I don't need it, not today. I'm going to work, and I'm go'n'a get busy. Two cars pass each other in opposite directions when I get back to the street. As soon as the traffic clears, I make a right and ride down the slope.

Cars are everywhere. On my left there's a storage yard and parking lot; on my right the service department of the Datsun dealer has cars all over the place with little plastic mounds on the roofs with numbers on them. The Mercedes dealer is on the other corner across the street.

Cars are flying by in both directions as I approach Front Street. Two cars have pulled up to the corner in front of me. The first one's going straight across; the second is edging over to make a right turn onto Front. I squeeze by the second and pull up next to the first and cross with him. Another car coming from the opposite direction turns left behind me, and cars start flying by again on Front Street. Cars are going in and out of the Mercedes service department. I have to swerve around a door that opens in my path. By the time I get to Pacific Avenue, I feel like I've been through combat, and I still have a way to go.

It's a straight run from here to Walnut, but the traffic will be heavy all the way. A young guy is shuffling along the sidewalk, staring blankly down in front of him with a big grin on his face. Occasionally, his lips move, forming words, but no sound seems to come out. I see him shuffling up and

215

down the Mall almost every time I come down here. He's obviously a basket case, but I'll be damned if I know how he got that way. I was cutting someone's hair who told me he was a Vietnam vet., and before he'd gone over there, he was an honors student and was a popular kid. It could be true. He's the right age, and except that he's got weird looking eyes, he's not a bad looking guy. It's sad to see.

At the corner of Pacific and Laurel, I get the red light, so I pull up and stop. Resting my right foot on the curb, I gaze over across the street at the Asti and the Avenue, a couple alkie bars side by side, the shabby antique store on the corner, and Atlantis/Fantasy World, the science fiction shop in the middle of the block.

When I turn my gaze back to the signal, I've got the green light, but immediately it goes yellow, so I rush to get across the intersection as it goes red again. The traffic on Laurel roars again in both directions after waiting impatiently like racecars at the pole position. Pedaling along this section of Pacific, I really feel like I'm in the thick of it, but I'm bracing for the downtown scene to get even heavier when I get to the Mall.

Of all these people I see before me, which one, I wonder, am I? Am I the old man who stutter steps along in stoic silence? What stories he could tell! Am I the young stud strutting, acting cool? Am I the kid with the telescope at cliff side looking at the marvels of nature? Am I the grinning lunatic talking to no one, marveling at nothing, or maybe marveling at everything? Alone all of them, and I'm alone. Of the ones I'm looking at, I don't recognize any. If I were in the Shore, I'd recognize them all.

I'm passing Joe's Barber Shop on the right. Joe's sitting in his barber chair by the window reading a newspaper. Occasionally he peeks out. His stare is so blank, he looks

One And Two Halves

like a blind man. Once I dreamed I bought that shop and when I went in to start organizing things, he was still there wearing his dirty white smock. The place was packed with people waiting for haircuts, so I started ordering him around, telling him to start shampooing heads. When he put the first customer down in the bowl, the dim realization (and aren't realizations in dreams always dim, even when we think we see things so clearly?) came over me that the shampoo bowl was a urinal. That's when I woke up. I've heard dreams are predictions of things to come. Either that or reminders of things past. I often wonder which category that dream falls into. Are things go'n'a get worse or have they already gotten as bad as they can get?

I can now see the entrance to the Mall. An old abandoned bowling alley sits next to an adult bookstore on my left across the street, the Pontiac dealer on the right. A three-foot-high brick wall next to the J.C. Penney store proclaims: Pacific Garden Mall; across the street, Super Auto. The traffic is backed up a bit at this corner, so I move up on the inside. It looks like all these cars are going straight. That makes things pretty safe for me. I'm abreast of the first car in line, and as he moves through the intersection, I move with him, and we're on the Mall.

The Mall was originally built to revitalize the downtown shopping area. It's probably done that, but it's also attracted a lot of weird street people, weekend hippies and transient hippies, too. This is one of those places where you see a beautiful cosmopolitan lady in all her finery, shear nylons and satiny smooth blouse and skirt, strolling along during her lunch break from the office, and she passes a squalid girl with matted hair and bushy legs and armpits panhandling for spare change. And of course, both cosmopolitan lady and squalid girl are so "hip" and "cool" and "far out."

217

Jerome Arthur

I remember how I felt just before I first started working down here. I was so anxious to get in and get busy meeting people. This street seemed so much like Second Street in the Shore. How quickly that illusion faded. I had the future all worked out. I was go'n'a go to the Cooper House and sit at the bar in the Oak Room and meet everybody there, and then they would all become good friends and regular customers and I would be as busy as I was down in the Shore, but I found out in a hurry that these people aren't that easy to meet. And why are they all gathered here? It can't be for the shoe shops and clothes stores, or for the restaurants, or even for the movie theater with its old fashioned marquee.

Less than two blocks to go and I'll be at work. The clock in the window of the jewelry store on the left says ten-oh-one. I'm late and I don't really give a shit. In fact, all of a sudden I don't even feel like going in, now that I'm almost there. Cut no hair today. That would be a first in about seventeen years. What a great idea! Fuck it. I'm go'n'a do it. I'll keep riding right past the shop, go up the hill on Walnut past the high school, cross Mission and back on King where I started. Complete the circle.

I turn the corner at Walnut, and as I do, I see Dave Raska walking in the front door of the shop. Bastard wasn't on time either. I stay on the other side of the street. Bill is talking to Dave whose back is to me. Bill sees me over Dave's shoulder and raises his hand, waving at me. I turn my head, look straight ahead, and keep on pedaling. When I get to Cedar Street, I look back after going through the intersection, and Dave is standing on the sidewalk in front of the shop waving and hollering something I can't hear. I wave back and say goodbye, but only to myself, and pedal off past the mortuary on my right.

218

One And Two Halves

The students in the beauty college on the corner of Center and Walnut are very busy cutting hair. The college is packed with customers. I cross the intersection, picking up speed. Now that my destination is really clear in my mind, I pump harder. At Chestnut, where train tracks run down the middle of the street, I cross with a city bus that's just picked up a load of passengers.

Now I really pump hard. I'm getting up speed so I can downshift in a hurry for the hill that's coming up. I'm starting to breathe heavily as I climb the incline. I shift. Fourth. Before I get to the left bend in the road, I shift again. Third. At the bend I skip one. Second, first. The high school is now straight ahead and it bobs back and forth as I pump up the hill. I take one last look behind me. The street is almost completely deserted between here and the Mall. A slight trickle seeps from some drain holes in the curb. The huge mortar and stone retaining wall next to me is streaked with water and moss. Way above it, rooftops gleam in the morning sun. If it ever gave way during a heavy rainstorm, two whole city blocks below it would be wiped out. It's not a very safe feeling being under it. Beyond the right bend in the road, my climb becomes a little easier, but not easy enough to shift back into second, so I keep climbing in first. I'm breathing harder than hell, and I've even worked up a bit of a sweat.

What should I do with my day off? Go to the beach? Go downtown? I could go back to the shop. Make the same trip again, only more leisurely. But what then? What will my wife say when she finds out what I've done? I can worry about all that later. I think the first thing I'll do when I get back home is fire up another bowl and relax out in the backyard. Then I can worry about what I'll do. I know that phone extension in the garage won't be ringing. That would be my punishment if I went to hell. To be confined in a room full of telephones that never ring. It was different when I had my own shop. I couldn't finish a haircut because the damn phone kept ringing so much. It makes me wonder if things ever balance out. I don't think they do, or if they do, it's not for one person only. The balance comes in numbers. If my phone isn't busy, then Bill's is. Or if the phones in our shop aren't busy (and that's how it's been for quite a while now), then they're busy in some other shop. And round and round it goes, acting and reacting, giving and taking, pushing and pulling until we're out of our heads with the confusion of it all.

I've reached the top of the hill and I'm beat. I shift into second where California meets Walnut. The wisteria's in full bloom on the wire fence around that beautiful old house across the street. I'm level enough now that I can shift into second and I'll leave it there until I get across Mission where the traffic is zooming by in both directions. Huge semis are rumbling by probably going thirty-five or faster. I'm beginning to feel lulled as I stare across the street at the red light. When the signal changes to green, I begin to move into the intersection, and damn it! I should have looked before I moved. My bike is hit in the front wheel and handlebars, and as I go into the air upside down, rolling sideways, coming down headfirst, I see the broken windshield and dented green fender of the car that hit me. And then it all comes back. All the parades and football games and schools and kids I knew and barber school and the Shore and Bernie and Vic and Diane and the hunger artists and the Mall....

II

One And Two Halves

The sun is out, the sky is blue, save for a puff of white cloud here and there. The white garage with its bright red door stands next to, but separate from, the white house, also with a bright red door. It is nine o'clock in the morning. A man walks out the back door of the garage with a bundle tucked neatly under his arm. In his mid-thirties, he shows the signs of impending middle age. Crow's feet bracket the corners of his dark brown eyes which are almost imperceptibly blood shot and glazed, and whose lids sag almost halfway down. His frame is still in good shape, but the skin sags slightly and he has a paunch. His dark brown hair shows signs of grayness at the temples. He walks around to the garage door, unlocks and opens it and disappears within. Seconds later, he emerges pushing a red bicycle out onto the driveway. The bundle he was carrying has been placed in the bicycle's basket on top of a book that looks like a magazine. A black elastic cord is stretched across the bundle. At the moment he begins to lock the garage door, a telephone rings from within. He goes back into the garage, leaving his bicycle with its full basket in the driveway. He emerges again and takes the magazine from under the bundle and goes back in. When he comes out again, he is closing the magazine. He puts it back into the basket and puts the bundle back in on top. He locks the garage door, takes a pocket watch out, looks at it, puts it back, gets on the bicycle and rides off down the street.

Traffic can be heard a block away. A bird sits on one of the three telephone wires across the street. It is nine-ten. Inside the garage, the telephone rings. The bird flies off the wire and two more replace it. The phone rings again. A car drives off down the street. It rings again. Now the original bird joins the other two on the wire. The telephone rings a fourth time. The next-door neighbor walks out of his house

221

and onto his front lawn, looks around his yard and walks back toward the house. Looking as he walks, he notices something, stops, stoops down, picks it up and continues walking back to the house. He vanishes within the house. The telephone has stopped ringing. A dog barks. A city bus roars by, a cloud of diesel smoke trailing after it. It is nine-eighteen. The telephone rings inside the garage. It rings six times before stopping. Birds are chirping in the trees and bushes and arbors of the neighborhood. As the morning advances, the wind increases. The sun rises higher in the sky and warms the day. Another car drives off down the street.

The neighbor on the other side comes out of his house. He has a crash helmet tucked under his arm. He walks over to a motorcycle that is parked on his front lawn. Standing over it, he puts the helmet on and fastens the chinstrap. He throws his right leg over the seat of the motorcycle, jumps once on the kick-starter and settles himself on the seat while the engine rumbles under him. Then he roars off down the street, which is absolutely quiet again, except for the chirping of the birds, the traffic in the distance and the ringing of the telephone. Birds are darting from wires to trees and back.

A small airplane sputters its way across the blue sky. Much higher up, a silver jet streaks silently through the firmament. The clouds have all disappeared. At nine twenty-five the telephone begins to ring again. It rings once and stops. A car comes down the street, pulls up and parks in front of the house. The telephone in the garage starts ringing again at nine thirty-one. It rings five times and is silent once again. The three birds have flown from the garage roof to the house roof. A car goes by on the street below.

The neighbor walks out of his house again, goes out to the sidewalk, walks along the edge of the lawn to the

One And Two Halves

driveway and then down the driveway along the side of his house. He disappears between his house and his next-door neighbor's. The solitary garage stands among all the other houses, cars, sidewalks, telephone poles and wires in the neighborhood. At nine thirty-seven the phone rings again. It seems to illuminate the garage: once, twice, three times, four times.

In the distance a car is heard revving its engine, "rrrunnn, rrrunnnnnn, rrrunnn, rrrunnnnn," and off it goes until the engine's sound disappears all together. Silence pervades the street once again. The silence lingers for ten minutes. The woman next door comes out the back door of her house carrying a basket of laundry. She goes over to her clothesline and moves along it hanging khakis, T-shirts, nightgowns, bras and towels. When she gets the last thing hung up, she turns the basket upside down and taps it twice gently with the palm of her hand. She then turns and goes back into her house. The three birds on the roof of the house have flown away. Two cars pass by in rapid succession. A university student wearing a backpack rides by on a bicycle. The mailman walks up to the house and puts some letters in the mailbox. At ten nineteen a siren can be heard in the distance. At the same time the telephone in the garage starts to ring. It rings and rings and rings and rings....

The End

1978-2019

About the Author

Jerome Arthur grew up in Los Angeles, California. He lived on the beach in Belmont Shore, a neighborhood in Long Beach, California, for nine years in the 1960s. He and his wife Janet moved to Santa Cruz, California in 1969. These three cities are the settings for his ten novels.

Made in the USA
San Bernardino, CA
10 January 2020